"In a novel filled with intrigue and mystery, Holland Kane has woven a dark enchantment—one you won't want to escape."

– Carol Orlock

"*Winter Reeds* provides a powerful first novel and tells of documentary filmmaker Mike Harrison, who moves to a remote northwest town to research an unsolved arson that left two dead. He's intent on solving the mystery—but standing in the way is a popular town sheriff who uses his deputies and traffic cameras as tools to keep outsiders from exposing the small town's secrets."

– D. Donovan, *Midwest Review of Books*

Also by Holland Kane

Winter Reeds
Morning Light
Car Palace, a memoir (forthcoming)

Praise for HOLLAND KANE

Morning Light

"Kane weaves a threnody of desire and guilt . . . David's invocation of Echo and Narcissus as a parallel to his relationship with Emily gives a pointed hint at the battle between lust and love that reverberates throughout . . . enjoyable reading."

– *Publishers Weekly*

"Kane weaves an intriguing web between the flawed, complex characters . . . story of loss, ethics and forbidden love."

– *Kirkus Reviews*

"a poignant novel . . . examines long-buried memories and unsolved mysteries . . . [that] comes full circle from loss and longing to passionate, obsessive love and, eventually, a sense of self."

– D. Donovan, *Midwest Review of Books*

"Part literary memoir, part poignant psychological drama, this haunting love story explores the secrets of attraction and the mysteries of obsession—a boy's coming-of-age, and one woman's search for love and success in a year of intense achievement and painful loss."

– *Aloi, Guiltless Reading*

"Kane shows sensitivity to language and story in this revealing book—I couldn't put it down."

– Ina Bray, librarian and former chair of the King County Arts Commission

". . . a modern woman's search for love and fulfillment, Holland Kane sheds light on the dark places our dreams can carry us, places we never meant to go."

– Carol Orlock, award-winning novelist

"A beautifully written novel!"

– Sara Strauss

Winter Reeds

"Holland Kane writes fiction that will make you think."

– Billy Squier, American rock musician

". . . filled with unexpected twists and turns . . . imminent danger . . . mysteries and corruption come together . . . the pacing of the unfolding mystery is satisfyingly quick and easy to read. Kane spins a fascinating web of discoveries and intrigue, and the surprises don't stop until the very end. A gripping tale of how some secrets can't be buried."

– *Kirkus Reviews*

DEER CREEK

a novel

HOLLAND KANE

rumor house books

Deer Creek

Rumor House Books
6029 95th Pl SW
Mukilteo, WA 98275

For more information about the author, visit www.hollandkane.com.

Edition ISBNs
Trade Paperback: 978-0-9858293-6-0
E-book: 978-0-9858293-7-7

First Edition 2014

This edition was prepared for printing by
The Editorial Department
7650 E. Broadway, #308
Tucson, Arizona 85710
www.editorialdepartment.com

Cover design by Kelly Leslie
Book interior design by Morgana Gallaway

A note on the type:
This book was set in Bembo Book, a digital-friendly version of the classic Bembo, cut for the celebrated Venetian printer Aldus Manutius by Francesco Griffo.

For Andrew and Lisa

In a time of universal deceit, telling
the truth becomes a revolutionary act.

George Orwell

Contents

Part Three

THE CITY

Part Four

THE CONFLICT

Part Five

THE FUTURE

Introduction

Two sisters, Rikki and Abbey—one given away at birth and lost in the foster care system, one pampered with love and privilege—find one another as teens, but don't know the reason for the deep bond they feel for each other. The older sister had worked Craigslist adult services, the younger one finds her sexy and bold. Their mother, a Deer Creek activist and the mayor's partner, doesn't at first recognize the older girl as her own daughter. Around them, the city of Deer Creek is buckling as officials fight for power and dominance. A police commander goes rogue and a whistleblower's revelations threaten to tear the town apart. Class hatreds, envy, family and community, love and lies, and government misconduct collide. Everyone, it seems, has a secret to hide.

I wrote Deer Creek before we witnessed warrior cops aiming their heavy arms at peaceful demonstrators last year. I wrote most of this novel before Edward Snowden's revelations showed us that the nation's highest NSA officials had offered sworn misleading testimony before Congress. I wrote the novel before we witnessed the spectacle of an American whistleblower fleeing the country to seek the protection of international human rights lawyers to help him escape American prosecutorial persecution for revealing illegal acts by government officials. I wrote it before Laura Poitras's extraordinary and chilling documentary *Citizenfour* hit the theaters.

We've learned something extraordinary from these events: essentially each of us is unknowable; there's always an undiscovered or hidden undercurrent. This book, a work of fiction, offers a look at two sister's lives lived within the pockets ruled by local government. Our local communities seem familiar, even intimate, but they are also unknowable. You have to experience it.

Holland Kane, November 27, 2014

Part One

THE PARENTS

1 JANUS, GOD OF BEGINNINGS

A sudden awakening registered in the tone of Ann's voice. "Yes, you'll need money to start your careers." She was speaking to her nephew, ignoring his girlfriend. The girl was petite, dark-haired, blue-eyed, and pregnant. "M-O-N-E-Y," Ann spelled it out. She paused to breathe. "A bushel I had already spent on your college expenses so you could then take a fling with your—"

"Don't, please," Tommy said. He'd taken a seat on one of the leather ottomans and Ariel sat on the other. Supplicants. They'd run off to Costa Rica, and they'd just returned. Like the rest of the extended Carver clan Tommy was tall, but he hadn't shaved and looked scruffy. "No one in Deer Creek knows that we have a baby on the way."

"Well, let's keep it that way." Ann Carver turned away.

She was proud of her profile, sculpted, slender neck, and her hair was alive with a red luster. She'd agreed to give them a monthly allowance provided Tommy focused on his career. She rose from the sofa and walked to a sideboard and then to the fireplace and then to the antique armoire to get her checkbook, and then she took a seat on the cushy sofa again. Using her knees to support the checkbook she wrote a check for a large amount of money. The check seemed to flutter with a weight of ten digits. "Tommy, I hate wasting our family's treasure. But in this case I'll call it well-spent family shame money."

"Shame money?" Ariel asked. "Because I'm pregnant?" She was jumpy and trying to remain still. "May I use your bathroom to throw up in?"

Tommy felt the air go still. "Don't—"

Ann was quicker. She shot back. "Having a child is no reason to wreck a man's career." She pointed toward the door and said the guest bathroom was the second door on the right. Ariel went to find it.

"You and your strays," Ann said. He loved pets. Birds, caterpillars, frogs. She waved the check in the air as if to cool it down, and then handed it to Tommy. "I'll get Ariel's baby off of your hands."

"Our baby," he said.

Her gesture said nevermind. "I've plans for you. Big plans. We're not going to have that girl stand in the way."

Tommy stirred. "I've asked her to marry me."

"Marry her? Marry you? You two married? Not if you want *me* to finance your career."

"Please—"

"Oh, *please*, my lady ass. That girl will drag you down. You'll become common like—"

"Like my mother?"

"Rest her in peace, my woe-torn sister. I had to go to court to remove her as a trustee of the Carver Family Trust."

"Why don't you like Ariel?"

"What's there to like?"

"What about your last two husbands? The men you wanted me to call 'uncle.'"

"They were mistakes that I've corrected. I had prenups. I kept my assets pure, the money separate. Whatever their faults they were good-looking and witty. I didn't want anyone going behind my back whispering 'who's that nitwit' I'm with." Ann fussed with a throw pillow. "Here's the bottom line: you marry that girl and your allowance stops."

Ariel appeared in the doorway and Ann motioned for her to come closer. "I hired Gayle Loftus to look after your baby while you're going to school. We'll need some documents signed." Ann motioned for them to get going. A limo had been waiting to take them to the airport. The lean driver jumped out to hold the door open for Ariel. He couldn't have guessed that his handsome young passengers were starting their life together fatefully troubled.

Once inside the limo Tommy shut the glass partition

separating them from the driver. The Ann Carver plan had Tommy starting his internship with Congressman Burk in Washington, D.C., and Ariel attending the Fashion Institute of Technology in Manhattan.

"She means to keep us apart," Ariel said.

He showed her the check. "Relax."

"Tribal bitch. She'd rip the baby from my body if she could."

Neither one of them was prepared to be a full-time parent. Ariel felt her anxiety rising, her bravery turning blotchy with doubt and uncertainty. She delayed starting school to give birth to a healthy girl at a Washington, D.C. hospital. Several weeks later they flew to Deer Creek to surrender the baby to Ann Carver. Ann picked them up at the airport and drove them directly to Gayle Loftus's house, where Ann's lawyer and a law firm associate were waiting.

2 A FRESH START

"What a beautiful baby," Gayle declared. She was white-haired and trim, energetic and kind, and had for many years worked for state childcare services as a foster parent.

Ariel was delighted. Gayle's reputation for nurturing children was impeccable. "I couldn't have asked for a better home for Trinity."

Ann shuddered. "You named her Trinity?"

"*Trinity* stands for the three of us," Tommy said.

"I'll notarize," the lawyer said to clear the tension. "My associate will sign as witness." The two lawyers laid out a batch of documents on the kitchen counter. Several of the documents were prepared for Ariel's signature and two were for Gayle to sign, and only one document for Tommy. The paperwork baffled Gayle. She joked about the wealthy knowing what to do and she was poor because she wasn't as smart as they were. No one laughed. She signed wherever the lawyer indicated to sign without reading any of it. The lawyer asked her to initial each page. Ariel signed her documents, initialing each page too. "What's this last thing?" she asked.

"Oh, it's nothing," Ann Carver said.

"It's an irrevocable power of attorney," the lawyer said. "You're relinquishing your right to make any further decisions concerning Trinity."

"Darling, you're giving me the right to do what's best for her," Ann said.

"That's right," Tommy said.

"I'm blessed to take care of your baby," Gayle said. She was soothing and sincere.

The lawyer, however, looked squeamish. He pointed to the stick-on red arrow indicating the signature line. Ariel added her signature and the lawyers left.

"Well," Ann said. "Let's go celebrate." She named a famous restaurant.

Gayle was grateful to have a job as a foster parent—it was all so grand and festive and happy. Yet she felt a premonition that her new ward might lead to unforeseen challenges. At the restaurant she kept tending to Trinity in a portable car seat. She didn't know which fork was which, and she put her knife down on the wrong side of her plate. The wine steward came along and asked if she wanted to have wine. Suddenly confused by the several sizes of glasses in front of her, she asked for coffee with sugar. The steward grimaced and made a rude little sound.

Gayle was humiliated, but she loved caring for children.

Ariel, too, had a premonition. She was advancing toward a great leap or a stumble but she couldn't tell which. A chill held her heart still. She reached to grip Tommy's hand under the table for security.

"Tommy," Ann said, "in Washington you'll have a chance to redeem the hog-sized bundle of money I threw away on your college education." Ann Carver was a patriarch and oligarch rolled into one. She controlled the Carver fortune through the family trust, which in turn owned OmniMedia. The money at her disposal not only muted conversations, but often revealed objects of interest and consumer privileges beyond ordinary means.

Ariel jumped up as if unleashed from a hot seat and pulled Tommy toward the exit. He winked at his aunt. "Be back in a minute!" Outside, Ariel stopped to breathe.

"Your aunt's eyes are full of knives toward me."

"She's protecting our family's fortune. She's tough. She got a court-ordered conservatorship to remove my mom as trustee before my mother died."

"I'll bet she stole your share of your mother's inheritance."

"I don't think so. But if she did, at least we're getting some of it back."

"By groveling?"

She pulled him toward the car. "I left Gayle's gift behind." Ariel had commissioned a silver commemorative box. It had Trinity's baby footprints etched inside the silver lid. They retrieved the box from the back seat and returned to the restaurant. They watched Gayle unwrap the gift.

"Oh, my Lord," Gayle said. She read the inscription below Trinity's footprints.

To the abundantly blessed Gayle Loftus,
Please take my love and gratitude, and this small token, a silver box to fill with your dreams. I will be in your debt forever. Thank you for being such a good mother to my daughter Trinity during the time I could not.

Love and Kisses,
Ariel Smith

The silversmith had reproduced Ariel's signature and handwriting exactly. Gayle kissed Tommy and Ariel, and promised to love Trinity as she would love her own child.

The following day Tommy and Ariel flew east—Tommy to work for Congressman Burk, and Ariel to attend the Fashion Institute. She shared a room with a classmate and on weekends either Tommy took a flight to New York, or Ariel the train to Washington, D.C. to be together.

His government career would soon take off. He continued to visit his Carver relatives regularly. But Ariel was unable to bear the sight of his aunt and stayed behind. Though she kept in touch with Gayle, several years passed quickly without her visiting Trinity.

3 ADOPTION

Ariel's long absence from Deer Creek had emboldened Gayle to ask if she could adopt Trinity. She was afraid to ask Ariel directly. "I love her," Gayle said to Ann. It would be an open adoption. Tommy and Ariel could visit any time. Mrs. Carver could save herself a bundle of money by not having to pay Gayle for Trinity's care. Gayle was as persuasive as she'd ever been, but nothing conclusive happened at the first meeting. Ann asked her to bring Trinity to a follow-up meeting. The girl had been an exceptionally good baby, fussing rarely, smiling often and making adorable baby sounds. She was alert and always curious. You could see that she was going to grow up to be an adventurer, a seeker and explorer.

Gayle dressed Trinity in an expensive blue outfit and took along her favorite doll, a cowgirl puppet. She strapped her into a car seat and drove to Ann Carver's house in Magnolia. Ann had set out tea and cookies and milk as she had on previous visits. She was extremely polite. The two women had passed for sisters, or at least half-sisters.

Money and privilege, though, separated them. Gayle wasn't comfortable with the grandeur of Ann's house—the handcrafted wainscoting, the custom window trim along with all the fine details so proudly displayed. The other thing was Gayle's inability to overcome a feeling of subordination. The more Ann tried to sound her out as a colleague, the more Gayle realized she was just another service employee who could be fired at any moment "without cause" as the contract Gayle had signed explained. A ruinous security agreement was attached. Secrecy was Ann's chief goal. Gayle had given Ann the power to forever impoverish her if she revealed the secret of Trinity's biological parents. Ann's take on genealogy was as rigid as any that might have been among medieval aristocracy. Surrendering a Carver-blood child, royalty in Ann's eyes, was against the grain, while imprisoning the child in a tower could be okay. Her lust for heritage ran deep, something Gayle was about to learn. Ann asked Gayle to sit on the silk-upholstered sofa. "You won't let Trinity spit up?"

"I'll keep her on my lap."

Ann looked at her watch.

"Did I come too early?" Gayle asked.

"Oh, no, no."

There was always a murky sense of taking up too much of Ann's time on these visits. Nevertheless Gayle explained that Trinity was a wonderful girl. "She said something like 'love mama' to me this week." The sound of it had thrilled Gayle for days.

"You're doing a great job," Ann said with an obligatory and friendly wave of her hand. "Terrific," she added with emphasis. "But it's not a good idea to become *too* attached."

"That's what I came to talk to you about."

Concern registered in Ann's eyes. "You need to be professional not personal."

"Not personal?" Gayle felt a sprinkling of coolness. Calculation wasn't her method. "Trinity needs me."

Ann was on the alert. "You want more money?"

"No, I want to go ahead with the adoption."

Ann was taken aback, and then she smiled. "Gayle, you're a darling, dear woman. I didn't think you were serious. You know, it's like, um, you can't just saunter in and *buy* a Carver baby. We're special. We go as far back as the Pilgrims coming here on the Mayflower."

The remark further confused Gayle. Then someone knocked on Ann's door, and two men entered. They were broad shouldered, with buzzcuts, tall, men in ties and dark suits. They came into the room and stood mute. Trinity quieted. Ann Carver glanced at the men. The taller one nodded in greeting.

"I'm taking Trinity back into my custody," Ann said.

That, too, was incomprehensible. Ann's body language nearly always showed a physical repulsion to Trinity. Gayle tensed. Maybe Ann just wanted to make amends and take Trinity on an outing?

The men took their seats at a dining room table that Ann had once described as Chippendale. They waited for a signal.

"This is going to be hard, darling," Ann said. Her politeness often came out in a declarative "darling." The broad-shouldered men were not smiling.

"I wish you wouldn't call me 'darling,'" Gayle said. She held Trinity's hand. "I'm not giving her back."

"Gayle, please. I'll take care of your financial needs."

"You can't have her."

"You've been a terrific mother."

"I love Trinity."

A minute or two passed. It seemed a very long time. The men were idle and curious. Ann handed a handkerchief to Gayle. "Don't weep, please."

Gayle wiped her eyes. "You can't have her."

"You can't just kidnap my niece."

The chairs and the oak floor creaked slightly as the men shifted their weight. They were undoubtedly armed. Witnesses. Authority. Officials. Several words passed between them and Ann. Gayle was too distraught to hear clearly.

"You're to leave the premises," one of the men announced.

Ann nodded and smiled pleasantly as she wrenched Trinity's hands away from Gayle's knee. The men then escorted Gayle to the sidewalk. The humiliation of that moment would simmer a lifetime—put out on the sidewalk after years of intimate service.

4 BETRAYAL

After losing Trinity, Gayle saw something incomprehensible in the classified newspaper notices. She called Ann. "You changed Trinity's legal name from Trinity Smith to Rikki Grover?"

"Yes."

"I don't get it."

"Just remember that our lawful contract forbids you to tell Tommy or Ariel, or anyone, anything."

Gayle was alarmed. "Trinity is now Rikki?" She felt a sudden shift in life's rhythms—the sudden losses and polite misdeeds. The lies, the bed of lies, the wealthy with their mattresses filled with lies. *How can people lie so flawlessly?* she wondered. It tore at her heart. "Why?"

"Mind your own business," Ann said.

"May I visit her? I love that child."

Ann hung up without answering.

A month later Gayle was thumbing the monthly child-care services newsletter sent to all volunteers. The newsletter listed new clients, and welcomed new volunteers. It listed Rikki Grover as a newly arrived foster-home services client, and included an adorable picture of the girl. Trinity, now Rikki, was a ward of the state.

Gayle felt a chill. She called Ann Carver again. Once again Ann hung up. But the next day Ann's lawyer delivered a letter by courier.

It was an intimidating letter, and it frightened Gayle. The lawyer demanded that Gayle change her phone number and reaffirmed the confidentiality clause that prohibited the release of any information about Rikki Grover, born Trinity Smith. The lawyer included a check for two thousand dollars payable to Gayle for "incidental" costs incurred in acquiring a new phone number without a call-forwarding feature. The letter demanded that she cease any further contact with Tommy and Ariel. Changing the phone number required only a few dollars; the rest of the money was spent to keep Gayle quiet.

SOON AFTER, ARIEL CALLED and discovered that Gayle's phone had been disconnected. She then called Ann Carver. The conversation was brief. Ann said, "Trinity is okay. I've nothing new to add." The conversations would remain brutally short on subsequent calls.

"I hate calling your aunt," Ariel said. "She knows it, which is why she's changed the phone arrangement we had to cut my direct link to Gayle. Ann wants me to grovel."

He didn't want to dwell on the subject of Ann. They'd bought a house in the lush Virginia suburbs and were gracious hosts to a growing circle of friends. Tommy was in fact no longer Tommy but *Tom* Hayden. Congressman Burk had promoted him to chief of staff. The power of government staffers was heady and Tom would have held on to the job. But Burk didn't plan to run for congress again. He promised to reward Tom's loyalty by securing him a top slot at Homeland Security.

Meanwhile, Ariel had opened a fashion boutique in the old section of Georgetown. In addition to running her shop she volunteered to help the Shakespeare Theatre Company, arguably one of the best regional Shakespearean theaters in the country.

"I want Trinity with us," she said.

"Why move on it now?"

"I'm pregnant. Maternal hormones. I'm wallowing in dopamine and estrogen. I want my kids. I want Trinity. Happiness. All that stuff!" They hugged and kissed and were thrilled to be parents. They began searching for a nanny.

5 BEYOND MALICE

Ariel flew to Deer Creek to retrieve Trinity. Loathing the inevitable Ann Carver must-have meeting, she didn't let Ann know in advance.

"Well, what do we have here?" Ann Carver said, unsurprised. Ariel was six months pregnant. "The baby factory?"

"Tommy told you I was coming?"

"He called."

"Where's Trinity? I went to see Gayle and learned that she'd sold her house."

"She's moved on."

"Stop driving me crazy. I want my child."

"Trinity is gone."

"Gone?"

"She's been adopted," Ann lied. "You gave me the irrevocable power of attorney to do what was best for her. You know how these things are, darling? The adoption service told me that the girls giving up their children are often ashamed to admit it, and the people doing the adopting often pretend the child is family, if not exactly their own. The confidentiality clause is very tight."

"You couldn't have—"

"I did what was best."

Ariel was stunned; she was barely able to breathe and felt slightly dizzy. "Does Tommy know this?"

"You can tell him." Ann Carver used the landline to call him. The device was on speakerphone.

"Hello?" Tom said.

Ann and Ariel both answered at once.

"Hello?" Tom said again. He seemed to recognize the voices. "Hey Ariel, hello Auntie. I can't talk now; I'm in the limo."

"I need a minute! I need a minute of your time," Ariel shouted.

There were shuffling sounds, the limo door slamming, and then Tom was back on the line. "I asked the driver to stop and let me out. It's raining here."

"Your auntie gave away our child!" shouted Ariel. "Your precious auntie!"

"I did my best," Ann said. "A wonderful family. Well-off and educated. We couldn't have done better."

"Adopted?" Tom asked.

Ariel cringed at the word.

Tom's voice faded. "You've never told us."

"There's a confidentiality clause in the adoption agreement," Ann said. "Even I don't know where Trinity went." Ann never bothered to learn where child services had placed the girl.

Ariel wanted to find a firearm, to look for a knife, to hire a contract killer. Instead she ran from the house and took the next flight east.

6 A SECOND CHANCE

A number of years later Ariel and Tom no longer needed a nanny for the daughter they'd named Abbey. The girl thrived at an expensive childcare facility, and then in private school. Abbey was on track to becoming one of the upper-middle-class children who would score high on SATs, and have interesting experiences to list on her elite college applications. Her cultural assets positioned her on the polar opposite side of Rikki's slide toward the economically underprivileged class.

Tom and Ariel remained in a committed relationship that was closer than ever, but they chose to remain unmarried. Tom Hayden, handsome and conflicted, was an excellent government official, and often impatient. He was promoted several times at Homeland Security and then something unexpected happened. He became the subject of an internal security investigation.

"I'm on an unpaid leave while they investigate."

"What did you do?" Ariel was stunned by the news, but tried to finesse it with humor. "Have an affair with a KGB agent?"

He'd been working with public utility companies to secure the country's power grid from potential terrorists and had left his government laptop, with top-secret information unencrypted, in his car. The laptop was stolen.

"Won't you get a second chance?" she asked.

"I think they're looking to showcase a teachable warning to our staff by firing me."

His guess turned out to be accurate. The investigation was swift and ended badly. His career had turned to dust. He consulted with Ann Carver on what to do next. She announced that his hometown needed him. He would show the locals how a pro could help them run the city, the region, maybe even the state.

Ariel sold her store and they returned to Deer Creek. Tom ran for a seat on the city council and won with several hundred votes to spare. The next year the council elected him speaker. Several years later, he ran for mayor and won. More years passed. As if in a blink, the Washington, D.C. years passed into memory.

In Deer Creek they'd reconnected with Gayle Loftus at her new home, in part because Gayle was the unpaid director of Deer Creek Arboretum volunteers, and Ariel in her capacity as chair of the arts and parks and recreation commission worked with the Arboretum and the Playhouse theater groups.

Whenever city business required Tom to travel out of town overnight, Ariel would go with him and they'd hire Gayle to baby-sit Abbey. Delivering Abbey into the care of the person who'd watched their firstborn was a fraught experience, churning Ariel's bad memories. She felt as if she'd abandoned her firstborn and she felt that Trinity was stolen from her. The two thoughts were inconsistent with each other, which didn't make them less painful. Trinity remained locked in a sorrowful silence.

Gayle Loftus, too, was a reluctant secret-bearer. She'd violated Ann Carver's draconian confidentiality guillotine by keeping in touch with Rikki throughout the girl's many turns in life, often despairing that she couldn't help as much as she'd wanted to help.

Part Two

THE DAUGHTERS

7 RIKKI

Ever since Rikki was ripped from the safety of Gayle's care she'd made up scary things to say that frightened teachers and a string of foster parents alike. She'd threatened to bring a gun to school, and she told underage kids how much fun Craigslist adult services could be. She cussed and used the f-word. Shuttled between foster homes, she grew up fast, mostly on her own, mostly alone, and then approaching seventeen she'd realized that she had only one more year left before she "aged out" of being incarcerated in the foster-home system. Though many youths her age aren't ready to live solo, she was eager to go. But then a happy thing happened: she was placed with the Clark family.

The Clarks bonded with Rikki immediately. Mrs. Clark brushed Rikki's hair and talked about etiquette and good table manners. Mr. Clark was a freelance news photographer.

He gave Rikki his ten-year-old digital Nikon and taught her how to use it. He also gave her a modest education in the history of photography. This was a life-altering event for Rikki. It helped to get the devil in her focused on things people wanted to see, to be awed by, to wonder and worry about. She tried several approaches toward a personal photographic style and settled, mostly, on staging and shooting scenes with puppets, starting with her first puppet ever, the one that Gayle had given her.

With photography, puppetry and stagecraft as her media she was on the way to becoming an artist. She wanted to document the underbelly of the childcare system that had imprisoned her. She wanted to show the edgy and dangerous slalom of her own path past a thicket of obstructions.

Rikki, at long last, had the best foster home ever. She belonged; she felt safe with the Clarks. They supported her and she wanted to please them by holding back on her bravado. She not only cared for them; she believed she loved them because they loved her. They said they wanted to adopt her even though that meant losing foster care income. She became, at least informally, Rikki Grover-Clark. But she didn't give up her hard-won don't-mess-with-me identity either.

Mr. Clark explained that he tried his best to get the shot that would "bleed and lead" on the front page of a newspaper. To get that shot he had to be close to the action. The nature of his work made him assertive, sometimes even combative. He'd been doing it for a long time even though the market for news photography was shrinking. He picked up extra cash by shooting weddings and private events.

The Clarks occasionally sheltered other foster children. That month they'd taken in an eight-year-old boy. One night, the easily frightened boy called 911 and said, "They're fighting like crazy," and asked if someone could come to protect him. The boy hung up and the dispatcher called back to ask for more information. The boy picked up the phone and said nothing—the Clarks were arguing in the background, upset by a mortgage-service provider unwilling to refinance. The dispatcher could hear shouting as the boy hung up. She sent a police cruiser on a domestic violence call.

The least pleasant of police calls, next to evictions and no-knock judicial warrants, are domestic violence calls. Most callers don't understand what they're doing when they call 911 to report a domestic disturbance. Many believe they're calling friendly cops to be peacemakers or ombudsmen or arbitrators, neighborly helpers, but the cops carry Glocks, pepper spray, armor, shotguns and Tasers, and if there's any indication of domestic violence, they come not to settle arguments but to arrest one of the combatants.

What's more, Deer Creek was unusual in that it had two competing, turf-battling police groups, a local one and a regional one, the latter nominally an interagency police group, the OPs as they were called, the Order Police.

The OPs were secretive, black suited, and wore triple-ought insignia. Their Darth Vader appearance provoked laughter and anxiety in equal measure. Ultimately they would be investigated by the Justice Department, but at the time these events took place they were at the height of their arrogance and power. They were more exciting and war-like than the traditional police force. The aftermaths from their raids were a frequent subject for Mr. Clark's photography. They were feared because they were unchecked and they manned their own secret detention facility. The OPs had in their corner a wildly enthusiastic and supportive political action group OPA—Order Police Associates.

The Clark house was on the edge of Deer Creek and close to the unincorporated sections that the city was trying to annex. The streets were dimly lit and the potholes larger. It was a jangly ride to get there.

Two regular police officers arrived at the family residence within minutes of the 911 call. A backup police cruiser arrived too, and, unexpectedly, the interagency OP SWAT team.

Citizens would later question the city council about the warlike attitude of OP policemen. Why would officials send a SWAT team on a domestic dispute call? Someone floated the idea that the Order Police were targeting Mr. Clark for selling pictures of the OPs in action, exposing them to public anger and rebuke. The OP spokesperson denied it.

A reporter said that it was a slow night. The OP SWAT

team had been bored, lurking nearby to pounce on a medical-marijuana grower who hadn't shown up. They wanted action and roared off toward the Clark intercept. Four fully armored OP officers with face shields jumped out of the armored SWAT vehicle that stopped in front of the Clark home. They saw local officers in the middle of something. They held back, assessing the situation. The woman who'd opened the Clark door didn't look abused. She said that no one called them and that there was no trouble.

"May we look around?" one of the local officers asked.

"Sure, we've nothing to hide." That was her first mistake.

The Clarks' rescue dog, an Australian Shepherd mix, whimpered and growled. Mr. Clark walked over and asked what the fucking ruckus was about. He didn't seem to be excessively drunk, but he was weaving a bit, and boisterous. The boy was at the top stair landing. The younger officer told him to come down. The Clarks, suddenly alert, feeling that their house had been invaded, asked the cops to leave the house. Mr. Clark became agitated.

"Sir, please remain quiet," the young officer said, taking control. "Who made the 911 call?" No one answered but they all looked at Mrs. Clark, who looked at the floor and began to weep. The boy started bawling. Mr. Clark became angrier, more agitated. His hands were brawling with the air in front of him.

The officers had no intention of leaving. They questioned the boy. Just then Rikki came home from a date.

Her furry jacket was unzipped, her white miniskirt riding high. “Mom, Dad, what’s going on?” The Clarks were the only foster parents she’d ever called Mom and Dad.

The older officer told her to shut up.

The lights inside the house were dim and the shadows deep. Mr. Clark was shaking a fist. He shouted that his home was his castle, and he appeared to be ready to hit the police officer. It was easy to jump to conclusions and see a weapon in his hand even though he was unarmed. The dog was barking. The flashing lights of two police cruisers and the armored SWAT vehicle made it look like an urban combat scene.

Three OP officers advanced, crouching low. The fourth OP officer remained behind to give cover. He picked out Mr. Clark’s forehead with the laser sight mounted on his gun. The other officers charged the house, shouting, “Go, go, go. On the floor, hit the fucking floor! Secure the dog, secure the goddamned dog!” A burst of automatic gunfire hit the dog. Its hindquarters crumpled, and it started dragging, whimpering. The boy ran toward the bleeding dog just before another fusillade killed it.

One of the policemen handcuffed Rikki. An officer pushed the stout and slow Mrs. Clark to her knees. She struggled to get up, calling for her husband to help her.

“Don’t fuckin’ move,” an OP officer ordered.

The boy was crying, Mr. Clark shouting, Mrs. Clark

yelling, Rikki, cursing, and the police roaring to take control. In this bedlam a single shot was fired. A single shot.

Everyone froze. The night was suddenly still.

"What the fuck?" an officer said.

The OP policeman giving cover had fired. Mrs. Clark was crying and trying to reach her husband. Many voices and cries and shouts mingled. "The medics are on the way," someone said. The medics got there moments later. Mr. Clark was pronounced dead at the scene.

8 ESCAPE

The Order Police had crushed Rikki's hopes of being adopted by the Clarks. As the long-form journalist and political opposition researcher Tag Orr will learn, the labyrinth of passions at work in Deer Creek has a cinematic quality bordering on melodrama. He will interview fifty-six people. They'll range from sex-workers to therapists to city council members. He'll meet corruption and innocence. Rikki's vivid life refused to conform to his usual understated journalistic standards. He added several exclamation points to his report, which he'd never done prior, or since.

The childcare authorities sent Rikki to another foster home, and then another. She ran away each time. They thought that she was too risky to be placed in a group home. As a last resort they sent her to the Stux foster home, which had been authorized to care for the most difficult placements. The Stuxes received a bonus to take on the hard cases.

Max Stux was a large man who worked as a guard for Yoshiro, a local business titan. Stux kept several guns and had a reputation for fierceness. His house was run-down, but it had seven bedrooms. The neighbors complained about the chickens in his yard, and about the three pigs that reeked, and about the refuse and old vehicles set up on concrete blocks.

A while earlier, a city code-enforcement officer targeted Stux and went to tell him that a new city ordinance required him to keep his grass cut to no higher than ten inches. Deer Creek enforcement officers, although not armed, wore several hats and the code was confusing. It was easy to nail someone for one reason or another. No one liked enforcement officers anyway. The enforcement officer was found dead in the slough with his throat cut.

It was a professional hit. No bullet, no evidence, no footprints—a wire had been used to kill him and the killer wore burlap over his shoes. The town whispered, and fear crept out in many directions. No one could gauge the truth of all the rumors. Some people went so far as to whisper that Yoshiro, a local businessman, had hired Stux to do a hit. Stux's neighbors were afraid of him. It didn't help matters that he was a passionate Order Police Associate. But no one had any evidence that he'd been the killer. The only thing that changed was that people came to believe that a murderer lived in town. Other than OP killings—some critics called them lawful police killings—this was the first unsolved non-OP killing in several years.

But even Max Stux wearied of Rikki. The word social services used at the time to describe her was "incorrigible." Stux called the state child-protection services to get her out and move her elsewhere. There were no beds immediately available and Rikki stayed with the Stuxes, waiting for an official reassignment. She was a month away from aging out of the system. She'd stored her camera equipment at a friend's place. She went back to the Stuxes to pick up her other things. Stux confronted her. She told him to go to hell.

"I'm going to teach you a lesson," Stux said, grabbing her by the hair.

He weighed nearly three hundred pounds. A blow from his fist crumpled her to the floor. He went to the kitchen and filled a Styrofoam cup full of gin and returned, cursing, because some of the gin had spilled. "The lockup," he said. He yanked her up by her arm and shoved her into the spare bathroom, latching the door from the outside.

The lockup was Rikki's routine punishment. Sometimes they would lock her up for two or three days at a time.

Rikki sat on the floor. She was an attractive teenager, passionate about photography, and recently involved with a new boyfriend, Richie. None of which prevented her from experiencing waves of despond that repeatedly visited her.

An inexplicable vacuum emptied her. The dullness was heavy; blankness dimmed her vision, her chest felt like a cave. She felt as if it were okay to die. She wanted to. In anguish she picked up a razor and cut her wrist.

She sat on the tile floor and gazed toward the ceiling, and then at the drops of blood on the floor. The Stuxes had spied on her, searched her room often. By inclination and by training they were prison guards. She was careful to hide what little things she could from them, especially the doll Gayle Loftus had given her. It was the most private, constant, reassuring, and treasured thing she owned: a miniature cowgirl puppet, hidden under the claw-footed wicker hamper in the bathroom. She couldn't leave it with the Stuxes. Leave it to fate, unloved. She pulled it free, brushed off the dust bunnies and held it next to her cheek.

Stux, buzzing on gin, was in the hallway again. He kicked the door. She felt as if all were lost. She waited to be beaten; she expected to be beaten, she deserved to be beaten she thought. Condemned, she cringed, and then something snapped. She jumped toward the door and locked it from the inside to keep Stux out. He shouted for her to open it. She grabbed a heavy glass bottle of body soap and shattered the sealed bathroom window.

"Goddamn," Stux shouted.

Mrs. Stux was now in the hallway, too, yelling to restrain her manic husband kicking the door. He smashed his way in. His Styrofoam cup had crumpled and everything smelled of gin. Rikki dodged right and then left. She grabbed her puppet, and scrambling, escaped.

9 BREAKOUT TOWARD LIGHT

Rikki's boyfriend, Richie, was working at a nearby sandwich shop, closing up just as she ran in. Stux was behind her, roaring that he was going to beat "some shit" into her. Her hair was windblown. Her white shorts were bloodstained, and there were welts and cuts and bruises on her arms and her legs. Richie threw the deadbolt on the door and shut off the lights.

The man kept bellowing and pounding the aluminum-framed door. He was not only big but also tall, a raging bull wearing a security guard's blue uniform. He growled and cursed and pushed his face against the glass door, his mouth open, teeth showing. From inside the store he looked like a large blur, a multiheaded monster banging on the glass door.

The doorframe rattled and rattled and the glass in one corner cracked, splintering and sending silver lines from the top of the door to the bottom.

"Oh my God," Rikki cried out.

Richie grabbed the baseball bat kept by the cash register.

"Whore, whore, whore," Stux shouted. It sounded like "warwarwar." The aluminum-framed door was a-kilter and a-bungle and a-breaking. The man's head was immense, eerily lighted by the street lamp, eyes the size of marbles.

Richie raised the bat and hesitated.

"Gimme that bat. Gimme the bat!" Rikki grabbed it, took a step back and wound the bat over her shoulder, the longest, slowest windup of her entire young life. The bat flew in full circles as she spun on her toes, unseeing, unthinking, wrapped in her inner tornado, winding up and winding up and winding up, torso twisting until she swung it in a final overhead arc and it came down on a slant, hitting the plate glass just as Stux's head butted the door.

The door exploded, and the man's head seemed to explode too. Glass pieces the size of pearls flew about with cartilage and blood—his nose was cut, his eye injured. Screaming and blinded by blood, he reared back, holding his face and fell to the sidewalk, his penguin arms flapping and then going limp as the mass of his body seemed to ooze itself flat, legs twitching.

Rikki held the baseball bat, stunned by what she'd done.

She stepped through the broken glass door, stepped over

the man's legs, stepped out of the hardscrabble neighborhood, out of her former fear-driven life, out of her unloved state, out of a covenant that had denied her safety and made her feel like prey at home. She motioned for Richie to follow her.

10 VAGABONDS

Richie had only a half-tank of gas, but the tank fueled an old yellow Buick and it held a lot of gas.

"You think I killed the guy?" Rikki said.

"You're not afraid?" he asked.

"No."

She had been forced to live in fear of the man in her house. She now willed herself never to be afraid again. Her wrist had stopped bleeding.

"Can I see it?" he asked.

The cut was shallow, hesitant, more like a scratchy bruise.

"It was a mistake," she said. "I cut myself in the bathroom."

"You cut yourself? You meant to cut yourself?"

"I didn't mean to."

"What changed your mind?"

"My doll, my puppet."

She showed it to him. He noticed the strings attached. "What's her name?"

"Crystal, because her heart is pure."

"I guess you've adopted her."

"I did. They would have shoved her down the garbage disposal."

"What are we going to do?"

"Let's adopt each other."

He liked the suggestion. He had only a room-share, and no family to speak of except for an angry half-sister who didn't like him. "I've heard someone say that if you want to travel fast you travel alone, but if you want to go far you go with a pal."

She'd been a solo traveler too long. She made a rough calculation. "Maybe we should run away? Try Seattle?" It was a shot in the dark. He nodded in agreement. They went to his room-share, picked up her camera equipment, filled his suitcase with his stuff, and took several blankets, a sleeping bag, and his camping kit. She emptied his closet of things that she could wear, shirts and a hat that made her feel like Bonnie in *Bonnie and Clyde*. She loved retro movies.

The heater and air conditioner in Richie's car didn't work. He hadn't gotten paid, and they had no money except for pocket change. He drove back to the store with the intention of taking his pay out of the cash-register receipts, but when they got there they saw the store ablaze in fluorescent light and cops inside. There was blood on the sidewalk. Rikki slid low in the car seat; Richie drove on, pretending not to look at the cops. Either his youth or his staged indifference caught a cop's attention. He signaled for Richie to pull over.

Richie continued to drive, driving so slowly that the tension could have broken a bone. He made a left turn and kept driving, watching his rearview mirror to see if the cops were following. Ever so slowly, he drove to the next street and made another turn before he stepped on the gas. The Buick lurched and rolled onward. Several thousand pounds of sheet metal rattled, the long hood dipping and swaying on shot shock absorbers.

He wasn't guilty of anything, but he had lived on the poor side of the tracks for so long that whenever a cop looked at him he felt as if he were guilty of something. He pulled into a parking lot and stopped. A cat meowed. Several late-night barhopping celebrants walked past. Then it turned quiet and Richie and Rikki dozed off. They woke early, shivering, but Richie waited until dawn when there was traffic in the streets, before he edged the Buick out, making his way to the interstate and driving nearly forty miles before stopping at a restaurant and gas station. They were low on gas.

Rikki approached couples, couples with children. She addressed the women first and gave the men a plaintive look, explained that her dad had run out of money, and mom was ill—could she borrow five dollars to feed the family? Richie worked the other side of the rest stop. He explained that his tires were shot and that his girlfriend was sick—could they help out?

They were attractive in their need for help, and each appeared more vulnerable when panhandling alone. At the end of two hours they had collected nearly two hundred dollars.

"Maybe we should skip Seattle and head for San Francisco or L.A.?" he asked. They were back in the old Buick.

She'd seen pictures of the rocky coastline and pictures of the rolling hills. She liked the sunshine and the youthful beauty of freedom. But growing up as she had, freedom was always elusive. "Are we going to keep wandering?" she asked. "I'm going to be nothing more than white trash like the mom who dumped me into foster homes."

"Is that what you were told? She was white trash?"

"I wasn't told anything, except some lies about her dying."

There was an emptiness inside her she admitted only to herself, and she filled it with bitterness. "She had to be white trash. Why would I want to know her? They kept tossing me out of foster homes."

"Totally, I get it."

They slept in the car for two weeks on the streets of Seattle. They looked for work during the day and panhandled in the late afternoon and evening. Rikki landed a job busing tables, and Richie got hired as a carpet installer's assistant. They each gave a false address to their employers and promised to get a phone. They cashed their first checks at a check-cashing service and by the end of the month were able to rent a room in Fremont. It was hand-to-mouth, but they thrived. Rikki got better at performing her puppets at Pike Place Market. This, too, brought in cash. She was also promoted to server. Richie's boss asked him to train as a salesman during the store's three-day blowout sales event. A coworker told him he didn't look old enough to be persuasive. But the man was wrong—Richie was actually good at selling. They were no longer hand-to-mouth, at least not all of the time.

11 HOPE

Rikki wanted a boyfriend she could rely on, and they'd started out thinking they were boyfriend and girlfriend, but as the weeks went by they realized that they were more like long-term intimate friends, even though they shared a single-room apartment. Experiencing sex with Richie, she could also daydream. Besides, they hardly spent any time together in the room. A folding, closet-sized door opened up to expose a small range and oven. The double bed folded up to make the tiny room larger. She worked in the evening at the restaurant, and she worked a few Craigslist nights too. He worked in the day and partied at night whenever he could.

Some evenings he had to work with a senior salesman. They didn't actually sell carpet in the showroom, the senior salesman explained: they sold home calls. If they could persuade a customer to let them into the home to show carpet samples, the sale was almost a sure thing.

Amid all this work, Rikki and Richie did something unusual.

"You think I'm smart enough?" Richie asked. He had a GED. She'd graduated high school early. That aside, they felt poorly educated. Rikki regularly served lunch to a teacher at the restaurant and asked for advice. The woman suggested that Rikki audit adult evening classes. She and Richie signed up for a class. They were sitting in the rear of the room.

Richie touched her shoulder and she turned to face him. Her hair was nearly shoulder length, her blue eyes deep. She wore a sleeveless autumn-cornflower print dress. Her skin had a pale pinkness and her shoulders, those shoulders he loved—the smooth skin, the warm touch stirred his heart.

The teacher read them a passage from *A Midsummer Night's Dream* and asked, "How do people know when they're in love?" Rikki jumped to her feet. "I know." The teacher ignored her and pointed to Richie.

"I don't know nothing about love," he said.

He spoke as though he were proud of his ignorance, as if he hadn't seen a book he couldn't burn. But he was putting on a show, ashamed of appearing stupid in front of Rikki. She raised her hand higher to get the teacher's attention and then burst out: "I know! There's something inside the heart! It beats faster. It's very beautiful! It's happiness and the hope of having happiness. It's a lot of things. It can happen to girls loving girls and boys loving boys. It can happen every which way."

After class they drove to Gas Works Park on the shores of Lake Union and parked. It was a clear night and several boats were heading back to the marina, their navigation lights visible. Richie and Rikki looked at the boats and then at the lights shimmering along the lakeshore, each listening to the other's breathing. After several silences during which nothing happened, during which Richie couldn't think of anything to say, during which time Rikki became unsure of herself, Richie said, "We would need a blood test or somethin' to get married."

"I'm not old enough to marry."

"We can lie about it."

"I'm not getting married. I don't want to."

The quickness, the sudden clarity of her decision disappointed Richie, but secretly, a big part of him was relieved. He had no idea how to manage a teenage marriage or how to think about supporting a family, even though he thought he should know how to do both. And sex was confusing as well, pleasingly attempted but somehow indifferent. "Are you gay?" she asked.

"How would I know?"

"Well you know, like—"

"It's puzzling."

"Bisexual?" she asked.

He shrugged his shoulders as if to get the weight off them. They were quiet for another half-hour, leaning against opposite car doors. She softened her rejection. "I don't think I want to marry anyone yet. Not yet."

She wanted to learn stagecraft. She wanted to be a performance artist and a better puppeteer. She was getting better with photography. She had looked into several Seattle schools and realized that they each demanded tuition she couldn't afford.

"Deer Creek is booming," Richie said. "They've got this Halcyon thing that's making the town rich." Halcyon was a spa-oriented health industry notorious for its controversial sex-surrogate therapy programs. First came the backpackers to enjoy spring-fed waters, and then came the condos, motels and restaurants, and finally the resort-style spas. "It's a growing market for the business I'm in." Richie was dreaming of opening his own carpet store.

"Are we ready to return to Deer Creek?" she asked.

"What if we killed Stux?" Richie asked.

"It was self-defense."

"They'll say it was murder. They'll try us for murder."

"They can say what they want. He was going to kill me."

Rikki called a girlfriend in Deer Creek and chatted for a half-hour. Nothing seemed to be out of order. No one had missed Richie and no one was looking for Rikki. They appeared to be safe from the authorities. At an Internet café they learned that Stux had died in the intensive care unit from a brain hemorrhage a year earlier.

"That's our secret," Richie said. "The only man who could identify us is dead."

"Relief? Should I feel relief?"

"Why not?" He let it sink in. They were free from the past. "Where are we going to stay? You know anyone who could help us in Deer Creek?"

"Maybe Gayle Loftus's place? Every Christmas she'd find out where I was pigeonholed and send me a card and a hundred dollars folded inside." The memory surrounding Gayle lingered like a lovely scent on a warm evening. "I'm not one of those kids who can remember being a kid, not all of it, but I remember her kindness. She's moved to a trailer park since. I have her new phone number." Rikki called. Gayle was thrilled to hear from her and agreed to put them up.

12 THE OP METHOD

Richie and Rikki slept over at Gayle's the first week. He landed a job with Fox Furniture after a single walk-in interview, and a week into the job moved to share a room with a Fox employee. Rikki remained with Gayle, and contacted Soto Cesar, a chauffeur, to get back into escort service. After a month her book was good enough to go out on her own. That's how she met Dr. Wilkin, who wasn't a customer, but well known as Dr. Angel because he'd established a low-cost women's clinic after a Catholic hospital conglomerate bought out the last local hospital and curtailed women's health choices.

A quiet man, unobtrusive, with bushy eyebrows and white hair, and a slow way of speaking, Dr. Wilkin was a retired primary care physician who still practiced part-time and helped to supervise the clinic. Rikki had used the clinic and remained grateful. When Dr. Wilkin called her for help, she didn't hesitate to meet him.

"I'm too easily recognized," he said. "I need someone to stakeout our spas and the hospital to see what news OmniMedia is suppressing."

Deer Creek news was dominated by OmniMedia, which in turn was controlled by the Carver Family Trust. If the news was unfavorable to Deer Creek it quickly got the kill order. One such item was Dr. Wilkin's "poisoned waters" preliminary report. The whispers about the unpublished Halcyon health report were rigorously censored because any hint that the spa waters might be polluted could destroy Deer Creek's chief source of tourist revenue. OmniMedia attacked every whisper, condemning the source, denying the facts, and pillorying the messenger. Electrical disturbances sometimes caused local Internet and cell-phone reception to go haywire—OmniMedia denied any responsibility—and city officials on the right and the left lined up like a squad of Spartans, urging beefed up surveillance and the prosecution of whistleblowers.

Rikki brought her Nikon to the first meeting. Dr. Wilkin hefted the weight of the long telephone lens she'd inherited from Mr. Clark and shook his head to say no. "The OPs will mistake the lens barrel for a grenade launcher and kill you on the spot. All we need is a smartphone to record video and take pictures."

Rikki joined a group of four to work on the stakeout. On Rikki's watch one evening, she saw something inexplicable.

An ambulance arrived without sirens or flashing emergency lights at the No. 3 Halcyon complex. The medics worked fast, loading two people into the vehicle. When they left it was again without sirens or flashing emergency lights. Rikki followed the ambulance to the local hospital. She got close and was able to photograph the two elderly health tourists. They looked pale and extremely sick.

All of this would have passed into oblivion, had she not been arrested for taking pictures. Not actually arrested but *detained* by the OPs, who also confiscated her phone. She was charged with disturbing the peace, handcuffed, booked, and released only after Dr. Willkin posted bail for her. Later that day the charges were dropped. The OP sergeant said, "You've got a lesson. Keep your nose out of our business from now on."

Locals called her treatment the OP Method. It thrived on anonymous denunciations, secrecy, and fear. But nothing was consistent. The OP Method never played fair. Public shaming was a favorite tactic. Women in certain neighborhoods were stopped randomly. The fact that they were women in a poor neighborhood was enough reason to suspect them of an infraction. If the OP officer found a condom in her purse or car, it was sufficient evidence that she was an illegal sex worker. She would be cuffed, arrested, a mug shot taken and posted on the Internet. Then she would be released without ever seeing a judge. The mug shot would remain online as extra-judicial punishment. The Deer Creek Blacklist, as it came to be known, had a few Johns, but it specialized in female mug shots. It was the most frequently visited city web site. The Order Police Associates were especially passionate in hunting Deer Creek dissidents. Rikki was denounced and questioned several times.

"Have you stopped using drugs?" one interrogator asked.

"I don't do drugs," she said.

"Lying to an OP interrogator is a fatal mistake."

She'd never taken drugs, which made her an outlier of her generation, but she hated the wooziness that drugs produced. Her innocence made no difference. The OP man shut his book, warned her that his questioning will remain on file and available to all policing agencies, and let her go.

Dr. Wilkin attempted to trace the two tourists. The doctor assumed they were European but had no proof. He checked with the receptionist at the No. 3 spa facility, who said much too quickly that no ambulance had been called and no tourists taken to the hospital. The OP Method was at work. The 911 logs had a gap, and the dispatcher said she couldn't possibly know what had happened without the log and the recording. Likewise, the airport limo-service operator said he didn't keep track of tourists. The Halcyon marketing group kept several private planes at the airport for high rollers, and the sick tourists could have been flown out in one of them.

Rikki went to the OP headquarters a week later to ask for her iPhone, but there was no record of its being confiscated or of her detention and arrest. The inter-agency OPs had become a rogue force.

13 GOING LEGITIMATE

Dr. Wilkin referred Rikki to a Halcyon psychotherapist, a well-established professional in the sex-surrogate spa industry. At the first counseling session the therapist asked, "What got you into puppets?"

"I love the puppet Gayle Loftus gave me, but my earliest interest in performance had come about when a social-services caseworker showed me a boy puppet and a girl puppet together. They were building a case against a foster parent I'd been assigned to a year earlier. Maybe I was eight years old at the time? I loved the attention. The grave-faced adults were minding my every word. It was on video too. I felt like I mattered. The caseworker touched the doll down below and asked, 'Did Mr. Grim touch you there?'

"I wanted to make the caseworker happy because she was nodding her head yes. I nodded yes. The two witnesses in the room took notes. They were scribbling like crazy. The camera operator had me in a full-face closeup. 'Please show us how he touched you. Use your hand, okay?' I froze. I couldn't move my hand because it never happened. I wasn't abused by Grim. They kept on urging me to show them. The camera lens was very close. In the end I didn't show them. But the adults, they seemed to be satisfied, whispering to each other. One said, 'We've enough to go on.' I have no idea what happened to the man."

"How does that make you feel?"

"Terrible. I've been threatened. I've been afraid. I've cringed. I've read the stats."

"Yes, one in five girls has—"

"I've been hit. I've fled."

"But sexual abuse?"

"At eight I was beginning to understand the disruptive power of sex, the fear of sex, the danger of sex, the desire for sex, and how to use it, too."

"Was sex forced on you?"

"Most girls—"

"But in your case?"

"I don't want to talk about it any more."

The therapist spread out the photos Rikki had brought, deep-focus pictures of mobile homes and their owners standing in front. The documentary style was different from the one she'd used when shooting puppet scenes—which she did with a diffused, shallow focus.

"Your lighting is so bright and yet so calming."

"I wait for the late-afternoon light."

"I like the way you catch the highlights brushing the shrubs and small planters and flowers."

"Oh, it's nothing. I help Gayle Loftus with her arb stuff. So I do those pictures."

Rikki's interest in horticulture was surprising. City kids dismissed "the arb" or "arbore*tum*" in a disrespectful tone. But Rikki did it for Gayle, trying to locate herself within Gayle's circle of love.

"Let's get at the 'it's nothing' part of your comment. You work very hard to get your photos just right. You take a huge number of them and select only the best ones. That doesn't sound like 'it's nothing' to me."

"Yeah, I work on them a lot."

"When someone praises you, can you just say 'thank you'?"

"I don't think so. I'm not sure I deserve the praise."

The therapist rearranged the photos. "So you never knew your mother?"

"The Wicked Witch of the West, in my case."

The therapist raised an eyebrow. "Have you ever been arrested?"

"Turning tricks?"

"Yes."

"No, not yet. Not for doing tricks. I'm not blacklisted with my mug shot on the Internet. The OP got me for 'disturbing the peace' for taking pictures of sick tourists. I'm all indoors otherwise. Referrals."

"You have a specialty?"

"I do myself up like Betty Boop."

"Men like that?"

"Some do."

"Do you like it?"

"I have fun."

The therapist pulled the photographs together into a short pile. "I work with several psychotherapists associated with Halcyon. Some of them do only talk therapy, some of them get into the sensual aspects of surrogacy work. Would you be interested?"

"In doing what?"

"Teaching men and women to get it on."

"I know how to do that."

"Yes, but you've always been the object for men's attention. We work, most often, but not always, with committed couples and in those sessions your job is not to have sex with anyone but to arouse them to have sex with each other."

"Totally, I can do that." Rikki noticed the framed *Home Sweet Home* cross-stitch alongside the therapist's diplomas and professional certificates of achievement. The text under *Home Sweet Home* read *Never Stop Fucking Me.*

"Oh that." The therapist laughed. "Some couples need encouragement."

Rikki wiped the corner of her eye. "I'm smiling 'cause guys don't want to stop doing me."

"You'll be under my supervision." The therapist paused. "There's something I want you to start doing for yourself. When someone offers praise I want you to be able to say, 'Thank you. I work hard. I did that. I'm good.'" The therapist paused again. "I want you to start a personal project to understand yourself better, a picture project to help you connect with yourself."

The therapist described a photography project to revisit Rikki's childhood to see what could be unlearned to establish a positive attitude.

14 LOVE CHILD

Rikki returned home excited at the prospect of helping psychotherapists treat sexually dysfunctional couples. She was even more thrilled to see that Gayle had installed new curtains. The next morning Rikki insisted on paying more for her room and board to cover Gayle's rent on trailer "dirt"—the amount Gayle needed to pay for the lot underneath her trailer.

For breakfast Gayle set out strawberry preserves and sour cream to go with the crêpes. Rikki admired a silver box on the dinette counter. "It's beautiful."

"I just polished it," Gayle said. "It's the most precious thing I own. I usually keep it hidden."

"Can I look at it?"

The suddenness of the request rattled Gayle. "No, you shouldn't."

Rikki was startled. "I can't look at it?"

"The box holds a family secret."

The weight of the secret was ponderous, a burden of undefined duration.

"You are joking?" But before Gayle could answer Rikki had the lid up. She ran her finger across the baby's footprints and read the inscription.

"I shouldn't have let you look," Gayle said.

"The girl is my age?"

Gayle nodded.

Rikki took a napkin to wipe her fingerprints from the box. "I can keep a secret. I'm keeping an appointment book full of them."

Gayle blinked several times.

Rikki felt it was best to move on. "Ariel Smith signed me up for the children's theater competition. If I win I'll be performing my puppets at the Playhouse Theater on Wednesdays."

Gayle remained distracted dishing up another set of crêpes. The strain of knowing that mother and her two daughters might meet at her trailer, and perhaps collide in some way, was a dangerous undertow undermining her everyday life. But there was no way she could have refused a request from the de facto first lady of Deer Creek to baby-sit Abbey.

"Can you go to the arboretum today?" Gayle asked Rikki, "to repot the baby century plants?" Gayle was the unpaid director of volunteers. She wanted Rikki out of the house to prevent her from bumping into Ariel who was coming to drop off Abbey. Gayle hobbled the breakfast plates to the sink and started to wash them. “I’m so distracted after my fall. Would you believe I even forgot to pay my rent this month? I’ve never done that before.”

Rikki checked her iPhone and scrolled through the coded messages. “I’m good. I can do the arboretum this morning.” She laid out three one-hundred-dollar bills on the dinette.

“You’re already paid up for six months.”

“Then it’s for next year.”

Doubt invaded the trailer. “I don’t want you coming home at two in the morning from one of your dates. I don’t want you hurt. I don’t want to lose you. I don’t want you missing.”

“I’ll be okay.”

“I couldn’t take it, losing you.”

“You’re not going to lose me.” Rikki wanted to show off what she’d learned auditing classes. “I’m sexually independent and financially independent, just like Chaucer’s Wife of Bath. She needed five husbands to make her happy.”

“Chaucer, who’s Chaucer? I don’t know no Chaucer.” Gayle glanced at the money Rikki had left on the dinette. “No more Chaucer, please.”

Rikki kissed Gayle on the forehead and left.

15 SAFE HARBOR

Unlike the resolutely upper-crust Mayflower descendant Ann Carver, Ariel bore her local celebrity with the humility of a slipper. When she came by to drop off Abbey, Gayle kissed Ariel on the cheek and hugged the child. "How's my beautiful girl?"

"Totally unhappy," Abbey said.

"No!" Gayle mocked.

"I want to go to Disneyland," Abbey complained.

Ariel shook her head no. "I brought her bike in the SUV."

"You should be taking me with you," Abbey said.

At nearly fifteen, Abbey believed that the future never stopped advancing toward better things, and that the future belonged to her.

"Where are you and Tom off to this time?" Gayle asked.

"A mayor's conference. Four days in Orlando."

"You're going to have so much fun," Abbey said.

Gayle smiled. "But *you* can help me at the arboretum." They unloaded her bike from her mom's SUV. Abbey mounted it and took off.

"What's the matter?" Gayle asked.

"I have to do mental triage every time I'm here. I keep ornamenting my past, saying I did what was best for Trinity. Adopted by a wonderful, rich and educated family."

This misinformation took away Gayle's breath.

"Our political enemies would tear us apart if they knew I've abandoned a child."

Abbey wheeled to a stop in front of them. Hugs, kisses, more hugs, goodbyes and Ariel drove away.

16 A BRILLIANT LIGHT

After lunch, Abbey was riding her bike outside Gayle's trailer park when she lost control and clipped the rear wheel of a Lexus leaving a parking spot. The older driver was distracted or perhaps hard of hearing, and kept driving. Abbey tumbled into the drainage ditch.

Rikki, just home from the arboretum, jumped out of her car and slid down the ditch. She took Abbey into her arms. Gayle heard the commotion from her trailer and came over. They drove the dazed Abbey to the emergency room. The staff ran a scan to make sure that the bump on her head wasn't hemorrhaging. They released her several hours later with a warning to keep a close watch for any changes in her breathing and the size of her pupils. Rikki cancelled the date she'd booked that evening and cuddled Abbey throughout the night.

The morning arrived fresh and breezy. There was no change in Abbey's pupils; the irises were blue like Rikki's. The alarming fears of the day prior receded. The two sisters, not knowing that they were sisters, felt an obscure intimacy, a need to stay within sight of each other. They held hands as Gayle said grace at lunch. Their warmth for each other warmed the trailer too.

"You're like a poem," Rikki said to Abbey. "Like a poem I can't remember memorizing."

Abbey studied her new friend's enthusiasms, her energy and her moods. Rikki's ability to craft puppets was amazing. First it was Punch and Judy puppets and then papier-mâché puppets, and in her most recent work Rikki was making wire, clay and epoxy puppets and documenting her puppetry progress with the Nikon.

As the months moved on, the two sisters often met at the arboretum. Rikki had by then won a performance slot in the children's section of the Playhouse Theater.

That accomplished, Rikki needed a stage to practice her skits. She set up a puppet stage in the arboretum barn to rehearse new productions—a compact four foot-by-four foot stage built out of corrugated boxes. Typically, she showed a new scenario first to Abbey, and then to Richie. She also persuaded Richie to help out at the Playhouse Theater, which would lead to his volunteering to help Ariel, and later, almost improbably, it would even lead to a small acting part.

These events were so fortunate in advancing Rikki's life toward happiness that a blissful normality settled in as she kept testing new scenarios at the arboretum barn.

"See," she said to Abbey. "These two puppets have a crush on each other."

"They're girl puppets."

"A crush is a crush is a crush."

"I want to be your best friend," Abbey said.

"You are."

"May I hug you?"

They hugged.

There were no perfect words to describe their happiness with each other, no pictures to illustrate it. It was glowing and immaterial, a doubling of intensity, a doubling of feeling, a doubling of intimacy. Something born of mind that radiated to their limbs, grew in their hearts, expanded when they met. Touch was like a scent—a forest glen, warm tilled earth, a fresh pond, orange-blossom, lilac and lavender.

"Rikki an' me" was how Abbey now started many of her sentences. Rikki seemed to be all the things Abbey wanted to be, informed by life, wise, kind, sexy, thoughtful, blissful, brave and confident—a model to follow.

Rikki's sex-surrogate work was offscreen. She was learning to be a guide, a teacher, a couple's hope for sexual reawakening, for resurrection.

She'd never considered sexual surrogacy as something that shaped the surrogate. But it did. It made her feel powerful, a presence, an authority. Her therapist had by now recommended her a dozen times, and she was becoming a favorite among several couples in the throes of the Halcyon cure for sexual dysfunction.

Most times she didn't have to remove a stitch of her own clothing, although she dressed special for each occasion, making her own sexy outfits to keep the cost down. She asked her clients to undress each other. They came from all walks of life. They were managers, professionals, officials, and the college-educated crowd, many of them married. Clients who could afford to pay the steep rate charged by the spas.

For Rikki, being in charge became part of her identity. She watched the process unfolding as if outside of herself. No longer apologetic, she was now more Lady Gaga than Eliza Doolittle. She was growing into the person her therapist wanted her to become. And she still worked with her favorite clients, outside of Halcyon. For these clients she undressed, and there too her approach was more confident, benefitting from her Halcyon work, where she'd absorbed a style that projected a cheerful sensuality.

On her own time, she was into electronic dance music, hormone-popping exuberance, rave and the delirium of youth. Energy flowed through her.

She held her sex work in a separate compartment, earning more money than she could've managed to earn otherwise. Away from Abbey she could halt any conversation by answering "What do you do?" with "I'm a sex surrogate. I teach people how to fuck."

Abbey was growing into her own sexuality, but she was in no rush to get there. For her, being childlike was an advantage. Her adoring parents loved to baby her, which Rikki viewed critically, as a way to keep Abbey from growing up.

She tried again to explain her personal photography project to Abbey. "They, like, I mean the photographers, they like to . . . okay, I'm totally losing it . . ."

Rikki tried to locate the exact words the therapist had used. It was fancy language, something about transference and reaction formation. But none of that mattered. Her personal project was to locate emotional intelligence, a way to unwind and construct a future to build on.

"I don't know exactly how to explain it. All I know is that the personal project is not meant to sell something, only to show something, maybe to say something, or ask a question, but there is no answer. That's all I know. In fact, I don't know. Photographers do it because they want to do it. Like something that's close to their hearts. Maybe something that's only accidental. It unlocks a closed door to our interiors. It's hard to describe."

"You're close to my heart," Abbey said.

Rikki faltered. Despite her growing confidence, she still couldn't accept praise easily. She understood several things by instinct. She'd been trying to save herself from the oppression that had settled into her bones and made her sick with maladies of loss. Her escape took the route of puppets and photography.

Rikki tried again. "My personal project is to reveal life to myself, as I know it. To model puppets and to photograph them in every which way to make us see the unseen, to let us hear the unheard, to make us touch what we've not touched before. It won't earn me money like fashion shoots or car advertising does. It's a kind of gift."

"You can photograph me! I can model," Abbey said.

"I'm calling the series *Sun and Shadows*, all about growing up in the Three Rivers Valley."

"That's so totally cool. I'll model for you, please let me."

Sun and Shadows.

There were shadows and shadows in the Three Rivers Valley. Anywhere you went in the valley, the branches and boughs and trunks caught the sun and cast shadows as the sun made its circuit from one side of the valley to the other.

"I want to do it," Abbey insisted.

The secrets Rikki kept in her head were tumbling about. What could she tell a teenage friend about sex? About selling sex? About the market for sex? The satisfaction of sex? About her own feelings toward sex?

How do you reveal your intimate secrets to someone you love? Her therapist told her that secrets could cause illness, disease, and even early death. A big secret is the king of maladies. Rikki wouldn't have allowed anyone other than

Richie and Abbey to come that close to her life, close to a truth, one of many truths.

Rikki touched every feature of Abbey's face to memorize it. The girl's mouth was beautifully formed and full and she had an air about her filled with love. For Abbey's part, she wanted to be hip, "Like you."

"I don't think I'm hip at all," Rikki said.

Outside of the sex-surrogate spa rooms where she flaunted sensuality dressed in fashion she wouldn't wear on the street, Rikki dressed carefully, even conservatively, to deny the gossips a reason to criticize her. Deer Creek seemed to know something about her, and disapproved of what it knew or had guessed or imagined, sometimes in pity, sometimes with curiosity, sometimes out of a need to spend a night with her.

"Rikki an' me!" Abbey said.

Abbey had never liked being an only child, a favored child, a pampered child, and a special child. Shelter, safety and love were treasures that she took in stride. It was all too easy and lacked excitement. She wanted to become an actress or a model. She'd posed for a children's clothing catalogue and had acted in school productions. She wanted to be bold, brave, a nonconformist.

Rikki, having lived a bold and nonconformist life—a life at risk—wanted protection and security. They were running in opposite directions to pick up what the other had discarded.

They each made separate notes on how to compose *Sun and Shadows*. Pictures grouped into public and private spaces. The public space was the lawgiving and rule-making space, the authoritative, the official public space, the city council and the courthouse, the public arena. The private space was wild and uncertain, sex and ego and chattel, property and pay, envy and hate, located in gardens and forests and parks of the mind, and motel rooms.

17 SEX SURROGATE

"Tell me about your difficult clients outside our officially sanctioned Halcyon work," the therapist said to Rikki. "Difficult?"

"What first comes to mind."

"Maybe the timid guy who wants to talk all night instead of having sex? I get the dominatrix request now and then, but I don't do those. The last guy I saw said he'd pray for me. I was both taken and taken aback."

"Did the prayers help?"

"They didn't hurt."

She was cautious and bold. Not an unusual combination. In her tweens she'd gone to a movie house matinee to see a Disney film and found a row that was empty except for a boy who appeared to be her age. She sat next to him. The boy looked at her and didn't say anything. He turned toward the screen. She made a small noise so he would notice her. He looked at her again and she smiled. He returned her smile before looking away.

She liked it when boys liked her. She was wearing thin jeans, Nikes and a tank top. The boy next to her was not moving. She felt encouraged by his steadiness. He flinched when she touched his leg, but then that too seemed to go unnoticed by him. More intently now, they both watched the screen. His zipper was a problem and she used both hands to get it unstuck. The boy took several deep breaths. There wasn't much in it for her, except in the excitement of the possibility of being caught.

The screen was huge but she wasn't aware of the movie action—*102 Dalmatians*—just flickering light from the screen. It wasn't so bad. The boy liked her attention, even though he remained bolted to his seat, his eyes locked onto the action on the movie screen. Afterward they sat together as still as two paws on a Sphinx. The memory lingered, one of several coming-of-age passages she'd described to her therapist.

"I was learning the rules, and the power of sex."

"Go on," the therapist said.

"I felt good and the rest of the world wanted me to feel bad."

"The rest of the world?"

"You know, cops. People pointing fingers at me."

"What didn't they like about you?"

"That I practiced sex."

"And it worried you that they didn't like you?"

"It paralyzed me. I even went to church to find love."

"Tell me how that helped you."

She did. What hardly anyone knew about her was that early on she was influenced by a childcare caseworker that'd told her that she was one of the blessed no matter what anyone said. It was during this time that she'd memorized Psalm 23 and learned to pray. She prayed that The Killer wouldn't destroy her. She pleaded with the Lord to watch over her. She hoped that He was looking out for her, guiding her past serial killers, past malicious sex, past pain, protecting her from the most serious STDs and the weird and violent clients. She prayed that the OPs wouldn't arrest her. She prayed especially hard when one of the girls on the street disappeared. She was a fast learner and graduated quickly to working only indoors, her prayers answered.

"We've discussed Halcyon several times," the therapist said.

"Yeah. It's a great gig. I'm not afraid working Halcyon."

"And legitimate."

"I like being legal."

"Do you want to get married?"

"At the drop of a coin. If I can find a straight guy to love me."

"Any luck?"

"My best friend Richie loves me."

"That's good."

"We're, we're, you know, we're not actually sleeping together."

"How does that make you feel?"

"I like guys making love to me."

"The sex-surrogate work—?"

"Makes me feel loved." She gave it a second thought. "One way or another, I'm always busy. I wish I knew more. The Masters and Johnson stuff. The Kinsey Reports. More about human failings that you see in your clients."

"I see social ineptitude, fear of ridicule, inability to connect with gentleness, premature and inaccurate judgments about oneself and others, sheer ignorance about human sexual response, embarrassment, and when it comes to the mechanics of sex, performance anxiety and haste."

"I'm never in a hurry."

"I have a high-profile client who needs your help. And, well, also, he's a little weird. This has to be more than confidential. It has to be top secret. He's a city official. It would ruin his career."

"I'm qualified to help." She was sure of it. "I practice good sex."

"I want you to help him feel comfortable with women."

"He's also gay?"

"Oh, no, no. It's more like, well . . ."

"Who is this guy?"

"The deputy mayor, Dustin Lewis, the civilian commander of our Order Police."

"I've never heard of him. I know Chief Clapton."

"Chief Clapton is the public face of policing. Deputy Mayor Lewis is the man on the rise."

Rikki's first instinct was to refuse the assignment, remembering how the OPs had killed Mr. Clark. But in the chancy world of sexual tradecraft she also realized that she'd hit the jackpot. "I can do it," she said. "I want to do it."

"The thing is . . ." The therapist paused. "He has to first believe you're a real prostitute. Not sex-worker, but prostitute. That's the word he would use. It comes with all kinds of different connotations. Originally it just meant to sell something, a tradesman sort of thing. Then they tacked it on to women and gave it a new set of meanings."

"I can manage."

"There's one other little thing."

Rikki waited for the bad news.

"He has to think he's falling in love with you." The pause was much longer. "I'd go for volume with this client—"

"He has to fall in love with me to fuck me?"

"Maybe not the first time. But get him to come back to you. It might be a challenge."

"I'm game."

Sexual trolling for a deputy mayor excited Rikki. A public figure. An authority. Beyond mere performance, she liked the game of seduction, the subtle wit, the unexpected humor, and she was good at it in the Halcyon program. Her new client was a departure from the usual mumblecore, married-guy profile she'd had to deal with.

18 PROFESSIONAL SPIRIT

A month later in the nearby city of Benson, Rikki was having a beer with Richie at their favorite bar. "The deputy mayor is a swinger," Richie said. "He hauls his butt a junket of miles out of Deer Creek to get it on with prostitutes in Benson."

"How did you get to know him?" Rikki asked.

"The usual Deer Creek way. He came in for a shakedown. Demanding donations from my boss to support the OPs. It was a funny scene. He had one of his police hooligans with him. Officer Hulk. All in black uniform and huge. This OP puppy wore his snappy insignia flashing like lightning. Lewis was in civvies. He asked my boss to make a donation to the OPA, you know, the Order Police Association. In cash, he says. Anything. A couple of bucks. He mentioned ten dollars. My boss takes some bills from the cash register and stuffs them into the envelope that Lewis can't see, but the uniformed Hulk is watching my boss every second and shaking his head to say no. She keeps putting more money into the envelope and the Hulk keeps shaking his head no. Finally, I think she put in five or six hundred dollars. The Hulk stops shaking his head and Lewis says, 'Thank you.'"

"And?"

"You don't want to mess with the Order Police or the OP Method if you want to do business in Deer Creek."

"Do you think he'll hurt me?"

"Jesus, I hope not."

"My therapist said I'd be okay legally."

"Your therapist? You're paying a therapist? You're upping your game in the Valley."

She felt a moment of pride. "I'm working to educate clients. I teach girl-like social skills so guys don't go punching girls in the mouth. I communicate. I teach them how to love me."

"Love you or make love to you?"

"*Love* me . . ."

"Sounds like a great gig," Richie said. "Do I have a chance?"

She punched him on the shoulder. "You're not even turned on by me."

"Yeah, but I love you."

They clinked glasses.

"You want to ride shotgun for me when I see the deputy mayor?"

He perked up. "Yeah?"

"Night work. Weekends."

"I can find the time."

"You ever fire a gun?"

"You know me."

"I'll buy you a shotgun and you can pretend you know how to use it."

"Me and the NRA?"

"You're my security. All you have to do is sit quietly in next room."

"With my shotgun. I'm on."

Rikki paid the bill for both of them. She kissed Richie on the cheek. "I'll call you with the time and address and room number."

That Friday she booked the rooms and met Richie a half-hour before her deputy mayor appointment. She didn't have a shotgun to give him but she'd paid for two connected rooms and arranged a room service dinner for Richie. She bolted the connecting door shut and told him that he was to listen and if anything bad were to happen to her she would scream and he should make a lot of noise and call the local police.

She left Richie to have his dinner and went to the Benson bar where she was supposed to meet the deputy mayor. She wore Lucite-heeled platform shoes, a thick gold chain, and a tight, short skirt. She'd memorized the psychotherapist's instructions: "go to the Wolf bar in Benson, sit at the end of the bar, and throw a big tip at the bartender, he's in on the game. Don't drink anything alcoholic and hold back while you're nursing a Shirley Temple. Wait for Lewis. You'll recognize him because he'll be wearing a black leather jacket with chains sewn into the shoulders. He's only five foot seven but he'll come swinging through the doors, the chains bulking him up. Let him settle in and let him have a drink or two before you approach him. He'll want to buy you a drink and you'll accept it. But only one drink even if he has several. You chat. You don't care what he's talking about but whatever he says you agree with him. He's the master and he wants undisputed agreement. Don't argue with him.

"At some special moment when you're feeling good, place your hand on his thigh and give him several supportive rubs. That's all you need to do. Please don't ask questions, anything that could put him on edge, just offer praise. It doesn't matter what you say. Praise is praise. We know our client. Don't take it as gospel that this approach will work with anyone else. Your professional fee and expenses are enclosed. Cash. Good luck!"

She took a seat at the far end of the bar and before ordering a Shirley Temple tipped the bartender forty dollars. The only question remaining was her ability to act the role the deputy mayor expected of a prostitute. Fantasy resided in the client's mind. She recognized him immediately as he entered. Just as the therapist had described he was bulked up, wearing a beefy leather jacket with sewn-in chains. Strutting, sauntering, slouching, he took what must have been his usual spot at the end of the bar.

She followed the script. They did the bar scene and then they went to the motel. It was missionary-style sex. Uninspired. Routine. Even boring. Richie, in the adjoining room, noted that nothing bad was happening. He heard someone leaving after midnight. His work accomplished, he was happy to go to asleep.

19 THE DEPUTY MAYOR AND RIKKI

Had Lewis applied his stealthy and clandestine leave-no-evidence-behind approach to picking up a girl in Benson, he wouldn't have seen Rikki two times. Each visit with a new woman provoked danger: the risk of exposing his official position, but that danger also excited him.

Lewis was captivated by Rikki's voice, the languid tallness, and something unusual happened that hadn't happened with other sex workers—he liked to be with her even *after* they'd had sex.

He went to see her again, and again and again. He couldn't stop thinking of her. First Lewis became comfortable with her, and then he admitted to himself that he liked her, and then he grew to like her more and more. He became a regular. A favorite.

"I want you to stay with me," Rikki said.

"Why? I'll never make you happy."

"I want you to love no one else but me."

"I can't tell how many women I'll love until the end of my life. You're a hooker and I'm a rent boy," he said, inverting the usual meaning of rent boy.

Forbidden sex aroused him. The business of nice-boy dating nice-girl sex went nowhere with him. His therapy, though, was successful. He could get it on with his steady, Kirstin. Once that was accomplished, the therapist felt duty-bound to tell him that the playmate he had known as Suzy was Rikki and a professional sex surrogate.

"It was all a set-up?" he asked.

"Most of it," the therapist said.

"I want her to love me anyway."

"The therapy was successful. You have Kirstin."

This revelation disappointed him but it didn't startle him. Pretense can be wonderful, imagination powerful. That aside, the die had been cast—he was unable to break the sexual hold Rikki had on him. He wanted her to continue his therapy; he wanted her playing her outlier role, pushing him beyond the authoritarian pattern of his everyday life.

For his next session he'd gelled his hair, and it glistened. Rikki caught his stare. She drew back a notch. He seemed to have assault on his mind. This wasn't the usual touching and feeling that she was teaching him.

"You want to subdue me?" he growled, which brought a grin to her face. He didn't want to let her go. He told her that she'd changed his life. "How did this happen?" he asked, gasping for breath. "Simple sex fucked me up? I'm into an off-the-charts crazy thing. I can't leave you alone."

Rikki, too, was experiencing something new. She rarely got aroused with her clients, now she was sleeping with the force, the main authority, the civilian commander of the OPs, and it excited her. A number of people cringed when they saw him, and some wanted his autograph. She felt protected, secure, and alternately, in charge. "I want to fall in love with you," she said.

"I'm into it," he said.

By this time Rikki had left Gayle's trailer park and had rented a house of her own. Lewis was sharing a bed with her and fit snugly.

"No one ever hurled the word *love* at me," Lewis said.

She was taller. She believed in simplicity, in straight shots, open doors, dot-to-dot connections, and direct action. She was also moody and impulsive. He wasn't impulsive, he was cautious. She bet everything on the moment at hand. He was a planner, careful. She went on, "My job is to cure your body's fear of intimacy. I'm showing you love."

"Screw love," he said.

She tried another position. They seemed to fit as if a sculpted Brâncusi piece. "I want you to feel my love," she said.

"The wicked things you say," Lewis said.

Anyone who got this close to her could see she was

attractive. The cops had seen so many girls like her, but few of them as pretty. She wasn't sure she was attractive however, not until she saw the longing in their eyes.

"How can you be sure I'm a deputy mayor?" he challenged her. "I could be a bullshit man."

"Some men are."

"A con man."

"Many guys are."

"A whacko."

"I searched your wallet when you fell asleep."

"You did?"

"I did."

"Can I get you to retire from being a—?"

"Sex surrogate?"

They nuzzled, puzzling it over.

"How will I support myself?" she asked.

"I can get you a job in the Deer Creek planning department."

He was skinny and intense. She was leisurely, and when clothed she was dressed in the best that Nordstrom Rack could provide a working girl. He spoke in paragraphs of clear prose searching for a teachable moment. She mostly smiled.

"It hurts me. It hurts me," he said.

"What?"

"To have you screwing other guys."

"It's my job."

"But you're unpredictable."

The rules might be broken, the ball kicked out of bounds. She might not want to stay in the background and she might leak the facts to the media. Her ambition was startling. She'd learned to make puppets not just for the fun of it but to be the best performer ever. She wanted her personal project to be shown in a gallery. She was a girl exhausted by her strengths. And now there was this new thing, the possibility of a mainstream social life with Dustin Lewis.

"I'm a fool," he said. "You've got something on me. You can rattle, tattle. Rat on me. I'm in this too deep."

"I'm your girlfriend," Rikki said.

She wanted more change in her life. The puppets freed her to live the lives she'd dreamed about, lives other than her own. Dustin Lewis, she hoped, would lead her in a new real-life direction. She wasn't going to be overlooked.

20 LOCKING HEARTS

Gayle Loftus's trailer park, the golf course, and the arboretum were within walking distances. The spacious golf course was crisp and neat and mowed, and not very interesting, but it made everyone who lived near it feel better about living. The arboretum was lush, and the barn was one of Rikki and Abbey's favorite meeting places.

The walk to the barn was exciting every time. The air was often crisp, and the mountains appeared larger because the verdant valley below held the park and the golf course. Each meeting was a bright moment. Something unspoken kept Rikki and Abbey together. They could stay in each other's company without a plan, without a reason, without explanation, over and over and over again.

Between them there were no doubts, no jealousies, no rivalries, no hurt feelings. Each wished the other good fortune without exactly knowing what that fortune could bring. Their extrasensory sensitivity for each other, a special need to be close, was wonderful, undivided and whole. They were sisters no matter what, but neither one knew it.

They continued collaborating on *Sun and Shadows*, shooting a photo sequence at the arboretum. Rikki framed the green color of the annabelle lighthouse-colored hydrangeas in her lens. She used a wide-angle short-focus. The hydrangeas had pyramid blossoms as opposed to the rounded blossom bursts of other hydrangeas.

"You're so much into fine detail," Abbey exclaimed.

"The details offer tiny blocks to build on."

Abbey's personal goal, almost a mandate, was now aimed at becoming as self-reliant as Rikki. But Rikki's fractured foster life had marked her forever. And not in the way happy kids grow up. She was an outlier without knowing it, forever insecure. Though at the moment they were doing one of their favorite things, sitting on a wrought-iron-framed bench at the arboretum and dreaming about the future. Rikki showed Abbey the interlocking halves of a Janus-like gold coin—the Roman god of transitions, of passages marked by beginnings and ends.

"See, it fits," Rikki said. "It means we are one."

"Where did you find it?"

"Ohh . . ."

"It must be expensive."

"It is."

They fitted the interlocking irregular halves together. Each half was partially framed and had a bail for a gold chain to pass through. Rikki held up two chains, one longer and one for the wrist. "You can wear yours on your neck or on your wrist."

"Which do *you* want?" Abbey asked.

Rikki chose the shorter chain. She helped Abbey unclasp the longer chain and threaded one end into the bail, and then placed Abbey's half of the coin around her neck and closed the clasp. Abbey held the coin in both hands—they decided that Abbey's Janus was looking toward the future.

Their eyes sparkled with happiness.

Whenever they were to be separated for more than a few days they fitted the halves of the Janus coin before leaving each other, and then they fitted the halves when meeting again.

21 A WARRIOR MAN

Lewis felt supreme at home in his man cave. He had a strong, resolute chin; he had a good voice. He could adopt a stern gaze. He had the appearance of a leader except for his height. He should've been taller, maybe five inches taller. He suited up SWAT and felt better. The full-body armor, the camouflage suit and mask, made him look as menacing as Henry VIII in full armor. He switched on the huge TV and played AC/DC's video performance of "Thunderstruck."

Thunderstruck, thunderstruck. He pounded his chest. Knee pads, arm pads, shin pads, body armor, a Kevlar crotch protector. *Yeah, yeah, yeah, thunderstruck.* All black, all dark, all ready to attack. He was fuckin' amazing, he said to himself and took several selfies with his smartphone, sending one to Rikki.

The glint in the face shield obscured his features as he moved to get a better angle in front of the mirror. He took several more selfies. He checked the crotch protector. *Genius is in the genitals*, Mussolini had proclaimed. But even dressed in his OP SWAT regalia Lewis realized he faced several challenges. He had to be careful how he appeared to others, not too assertive, not too arrogant. He had to know whom to inform, whom to appease, whom to mislead and whom to betray. In all of this he had to appear evenhanded and fair, caring, careful and unselfish.

The balancing act was getting on his nerves. He found refuge in his man cave, his "will to power" room. He put away his SWAT armor and felt diminished, ordinary again—shrimpo, shorty, no one would take him for a menacing force, a powerful man. He loved suiting up. He loved the weight of it, the heft of it, the way it made him walk, a powerful, swaying walk. Big man Lewis. Ominous Lewis. Powerful Lewis. He deserved his own pantheon. His bulked-up shoulders tilting from side to side, a human tank, a warrior, terrified the prisoners he held in the OP detention center.

The thing about Rikki was that she reinforced his image of himself as a player, a strong leader. Before Rikki he'd been clumsy with women, and then there was the other thing, his inability to up his game in normal situations. But now, as deputy mayor, as the commander of the Order Police, he had an aura. Under Rikki's approving gaze he saw himself in vivid colors. He was a godlike guru, and she the willing disciple.

He quoted *On the Genealogy of Morals* to explain himself: "... the meaning of all culture is the reduction of the beast of prey 'man' to a tame and civilized animal, a domestic animal." He thumped his chest to prove to himself that he was an untamed man, a predator, king of the jungle. "I'm gonna make this half-assed burg into Century City! It'll live for a thousand years after I die." He'd launched his career as a city planner. In addition to becoming the chief of planning and deputy mayor, he'd wrestled the role of a lifetime as the civilian commander of the Order Police. Appointed as overseer to reign in the SWAT cops, he'd expanded their arrogant franchise.

"I THINK DUSTIN LEWIS is having me followed," Rikki said to Richie. They were at an out-of-the-way bar. It was early in the evening and no one was dancing.

"Are you still working with Dr. Wilkin?"

"Whenever he needs me."

"Is he getting anywhere in his research?"

"Bad news. It's all bad news. He sent additional spa water samples to be analyzed outside the state."

"What makes you think Lewis would tolerate you helping his enemy?"

"I'm careful. I learned early on how to spot police spies.

I learned early on not to call the cops for help. We're as often the victims of police violence as we are victims of client violence. It was the Green River serial killer, Gary Ridgway, who said he was doing the police a favor by killing sex workers."

"If you were living in Russia he'd have you shot, or he would look the other way when someone else does you in."

"I hope not."

"What's this Operation Purification he's launched with the Halcyon Business Watch?"

"He wants to have all the girls off the streets, or working for Halcyon."

"Either, or?"

"Either Halcyon or jail. The girls are driving Halcyon prices down."

"He doesn't like that?"

"Halcyon hates the competition."

"Does that make you uncomfortable?"

"I know those girls, and only a few of them are tens."

"Tens?"

"Halcyon hires you on a scale. You have to scale as a ten to work at Halcyon. You have to have the right proportions, height, weight, accent, light skin color. I signed a contract that says if my weight goes up by more than three percent they can dock twenty percent of my pay."

"How many girls do you know that are tens?"

"One out of ten."

"They don't get to work at Halcyon?"

"No. They work the streets, the motels, or freelance at home. The Halcyon Business Watch is funding the Operation Purification to stop them."

"Purification?"

"That's what they call it."

"How are your friends handling it?"

"How does it look like to you?"

"To me? It looks like Operation Purification is straddling the usual hypocrisy between making money and remaining pious. Lewis must lead a charmed life as the town's moral leader."

"I worry about my friends but I can't live outside of my relationship with Lewis. He protects me."

"Don't let him catch you helping Dr. Wilkin."

They had their elbows resting up on the bar. It was a quiet bar and the quietness was the reason they liked it. Their affection for each other escaped traditional gender roles. Neither one was competing to capture the other to the exclusion of all others.

"'All's fair in love and war'?" Richie asked.

"How stupid is that?"

"I didn't say I'm smart."

"I didn't accuse you of anything."

They needed each other.

22 PLAYFULNESS

Her reservations aside, Rikki was awed by Lewis. His mind was either clean-cut or tawdry, his actions worked to uphold the common good or were disreputable. Once thing was for sure, his causes were larger than her own relationship needs. Her man was powerful. She'd never met a man who spouted Nietzsche to her. He quoted from *Thus Spoke Zarathustra*: "Two things a genuine man wants: danger and play. Therefore he wants woman, as the most dangerous plaything."

A willing plaything, Rikki thought.

In her sex-surrogate work, she'd discovered that many women liked domination-and-submission games, none of which fit neatly into marriage and the childcare paradigm. The hunt is always exciting, the submission sometimes appealing to men and satisfying for women. What part was culture, and what part was gender, what part primeval, remained confusing.

Rikki played her smart card: "You're, like, um, you like a radical-reactionary girl like me?"

Lewis had to think about it.

He was proud of his a reputation as the most repressive law-enforcement official the region had ever seen. Except he didn't think of himself as repressive; he believed he was forceful, faithful, honest and true. Everyone in town knew that he ran a smooth surveillance operation.

He was working to centralize government spying—in his words "to make privacy safe." As part of Operation Purification he'd launched a war on privacy. Privacy, like government-owned grazing land, was too valuable to leave untended. It had to be controlled—rationed and regulated, leased in small segments.

Rikki's stomach did a little flip. Her lover was omnipotent. He knew the town's secrets, its loyalties, sins, and betrayals. She loved dominant and forceful men, heroes.

"In the Clark home I loved watching old movies, westerns." She named them: *High Noon* with Gary Cooper, *The Searchers* with John Wayne, *Shane* with Alan Ladd. She would have liked cowgirl films too, but there were so few she hadn't see any. Her movie experiences had taught her several lessons, one of which was that the saloon girls had more fun than the women on the farm with several children hanging on to them. She wasn't going to become one of those women.

But early on she had loved the sisters in Louisa May Alcott's *Little Women*, even though her fantasies featured mostly strong men. Things got confusing. She also liked strong women. For a while she was into retro *Tarzan* movies with Johnny Weissmuller, though in no mood to be Jane. Now, belatedly, she was drifting toward the cultural changes seeded by early feminists and preferred *The Hunger Games*.

She was in charge of herself. Her product was exquisite. Her work was reliable. Her ability to seduce was on sale. She could excite men and seduce women, satisfy both. Her instincts moved her toward freedom and liberty, but she subordinated that to accommodate Lewis.

These conflicts aside, she had the heart of someone who couldn't let go. She couldn't leave her doll behind to be crushed by Stux and she couldn't imagine leaving her own child in a foster home. She was adventurous and romantic, idealistic and doggedly pedestrian, practical and totally wild. She wouldn't have it any other way.

23 THE COMMANDER

Before his self-directed transformation into a lover and leader, Lewis led a modest life dealing with sign codes, mobile-home zoning, the number of chickens a residential house was allowed to keep—it all landed on his desk, an unheralded city employee. The technocrat. A code-writing guy and PowerPoint city council presenter. He was a professional on a high civil-service rung but invisible to most, practicing his profession in a safe buffer zone of public indifference.

Lewis's core belief was that he was a creator, a great builder, even a power builder like the celebrated, criticized, contentious and late New York City planner Robert Moses. He chafed at limitations imposed on his authority and wished he were as free as Baron Haussmann, the planner who had redesigned Paris for Napoleon III.

He complained to Rikki that he needed a Napoleon to back him up, but he had only Tom Hayden, a scion of the Carver Family Trust, who in Lewis's opinion was a dilettante playing at politics.

The Carver family used OmniMedia's clout to buy Hayden the mayor's office. The company owned five radio stations, a popular cable-TV channel and a local TV station, as well as a moribund newspaper, and *Focus*, an outdoor advertising company. The Valley was as near a totalitarian media fiefdom as possible in the otherwise porous social media world. It was hard to imagine anyone controlling so much access to local news, but for all practical purposes, the Carver Trust did.

That in itself was sufficient for Lewis to dislike Hayden. Lewis, though, carried his bitter grudge much further. City work brought Lewis his paycheck but didn't pay him in millions, or even close to the private-industry salary that the mayor's private-industry majordomo, John Foster, OmniMedia CEO and another beneficiary of the Carver Family Trust, was rumored to earn.

Lewis felt as prickly as a piece of barbed wire, agitated. He called Rikki again. Her voice-mail was full. It annoyed him that it was full. Where the hell was she? He felt uneasy, his leg muscles twitching. He had gotten her a job in the planning department but he worried, too, that she might still be working the trade on the side. Halcyon surrogacy work had been about money—he could accept that—the high quality of money. It spelled freedom, independence, shopping at the mall. He called her again and left a message. "Where the hell are you?"

Part Three

THE CITY

24 THE MAYOR

Tom Hayden liked being mayor but he had a problem. Aside from Ariel and Abbey, he wasn't sure if anyone loved him. The citywide staff layoff notices had gone out. Everyone was pissed. The firefighters were mad at him, the city cops hated him, and the teachers wanted to hang him. He'd tried to do the right thing and now this mess. The city's revenues had collapsed.

The Canadians weren't coming in droves to shop as they had before. Where the hell were those Canucks? Nesting in Vancouver? Canoodling with their evergreen trees?

Deer Creek used to attract shoppers from as far as the province of Alberta—all those tourists eager to blow their money at the Deer Creek Mall. Even the local car buyers were holding back on purchases. The sales tax levied on vehicle sales amounted to a quarter of the city's revenue. And to cap it all off, Dr. Wilkin's secret Halcyon report sat on his desk, threatening Deer Creek's existence. How the hell was he expected to run a city with no money coming in?

It was the Great Recession. The crises made him wonder why he had chosen public service. He could've made a killing in the private sector. He could've been a hedge fund manager protecting the wealthy. He could've screwed people by trading derivatives that went flat, made a fortune buying up annuities that collapsed. He could've fucked mom-and-pop mortgage payers going into foreclosure. He could've made millions and millions in the private sector like his Carver relatives. He could have. Instead, he had followed his misguided idealism and had sacrificed himself to serve the public on a mayor's salary, a hundred thousand dollars and benefits.

And what did he get for his service? Hate mail and loathsome citizen comments at council meetings. The recall effort had fizzled but the majority of the business crowd still hated him, and the progressives who had supported him had abandoned him. His deputy mayor, whom he had trusted until recently, was going weird on him too, fanatical, riding roughshod and untouched as the commander of the Order Police.

At council meetings Lewis's gestures had become more flamboyant, his hand thrust upward, his head shaking furiously. He'd even started to grow his hair longer, a lock of hair falling over his furrowed brow. At executive meetings Lewis was the first to propose the gut punch, the kick to the groin, the knife to the jugular. A war hawk for sure.

But then, every mayor needs an in-house ass-kicker to snap the staff into line. The voters had elected Hayden to make the city more efficient and he'd tried to accomplish that, causing resentment. Several department managers acted as if their fingers were frozen in dry ice and incapable of doing things for the city without extra staff help—it had been a long time since private-industry managers had the luxury of paying for so much secretarial and clerical staff to sit around and admire their bosses.

Hayden imagined a city-owned hot-dog stand with his city staff in charge. First, there would be a dedicated bun splitter, then a hot-dog handler with tongs, a ketchup staffer to squirt, a relish staffer to dot the foul green stuff, a mustard staffer to slather on the deli yellow, an onion man with an OSHA-approved breathing apparatus to keep from crying, and a sauerkraut man too—the hot dog would be cold by the time it got to him and would cost seventy-five dollars.

Lewis had volunteered for the ass-kicker job, eager to be the whip. But Hayden had made a mistake by appointing him as the civilian overseer of the police with the hope that he would rein in the wild ones. Instead, Lewis took the proverbial inch and marched it a mile, a turf master, persuading city and county legislators to fund a separate and powerful interagency police unit—the Order Police that reported directly to the "deputy mayor for safety" whose authority sidestepped the mayor. He had rebranded himself. He believed in "suspicionless" surveillance. His highway interdiction and private intelligence operation included Black Asphalt surveillance and Desert Snow training. He ignored the probable cause law that required police to have a good reason to stop somebody to question them. But he expanded the civil forfeiture law passed to seize a drug lord's illegal millions to take down mom and pop food truck owners carrying cash. He seized property without going to court. One grandma was left at the side of the road after her truck was taken because the OP found her grandson's marijuana joint underneath the floor mat. The truck was auctioned and the money deposited in the OP account. Lewis got away with this outrage. This alarmed Police Chief Clapton, whose authority had been trampled.

Hayden was distracted, on edge. A palace coup was brewing. His staff was out to get him. He checked the finance director's revenue report. The traffic light camera revenue was down a million bucks. A million fucking bucks short? Why didn't they warn him six months ago? Even his executive secretary was acting strange, as if Hayden had murdered the city singlehandedly.

25 INVESTIGATING DEER CREEK

The investigator Tag Orr had never been a victim of romanticism. He had the solid heartbeat of a skeptic. City officials didn't like it that he was hanging around again, checking the city's vital signs. He wasn't a detective or a private investigator in the traditional sense, and he had stopped carrying a gun after he'd left government service. He was an opposition researcher, an "oppo" guy, a political operative hired to unearth hidden agendas. He wasn't looking for lies, although political lies were abundant. His job was to document the truth that might embarrass a candidate running for office.

His current employer, a mysterious client, camouflaged his voice and had instructed Orr to use a "burner"—a throwaway cell phone—to negotiate the deal at a hefty fee paid in three installments. The first installment didn't come in the mail. It was delivered in cash, in a plastic Macy's bag left on his Philadelphia porch. That in itself was enough to make Orr want the Deer Creek job—he wanted to discover the identity of his employer.

Orr's first report was delivered at a dead drop, and a second cash installment arrived. Whoever wanted the research on Deer Creek also wanted to remain nameless. Orr's client had perfect and untraceable deniability—even Orr didn't know his identity.

He puzzled over the details he knew. Each political community was a social puzzle. According to rumor, the mayor, the city's most famous bachelor, had fathered unclaimed children. This rumor was a vote-killer. People said he was wealthy enough to live by his own social rules, flouting a conventional relationship by not marrying. This ho-hum arrangement might have gotten a wink in most other communities, but in a city where sixty percent of voters attended church it was politically damaging.

Deer Creek wasn't New York City or Seattle, or Portland. Although it was a midsize city, its moral and social codes could have fit snugly into a small town. Orr noted that plainclothes officers occasionally escorted Abbey at public events. He also noticed that John Foster, the young OmniMedia CEO and Hayden's privately paid chief of staff, spent a good amount of time looking out for the girl. Questions abounded however. There's nothing more gleefully fun than tearing into a politician's private life when he's caught with his pants down. Foster had been hired to protect his boss, thus he announced that the mayor was unmarried because he was faithfully married to the people of Deer Creek.

Married to all those people?

Hayden was so charming that even voters who disliked him often voted for him. No one is perfect, the townies philosophized.

Besides, Hayden had worked feverishly to raise the town's economic profile. He'd backed Halcyon as a world-class health destination. He pushed for Halcyon Annex mid-rises and brought high-income wages to Deer Creek. His popularity skyrocketed with Halcyon's success. His wish to "make Deer Creek famous" by incorporating and gentrifying the outlying districts to give Halcyon more "elbow room" resonated among many voters. The locals liked the idea of being part of something bigger. Small was no longer hip and Hayden was making Deer Creek safe for large-scale development.

Originally a working-class town—predominantly white, some Hispanic, a little Asian, some Native Americans, and a sprinkling of blacks—it wasn't a city that attracted young professionals except for those employed by the Halcyon health industry. That aside, the people there were hardworking and committed to traditional values, hopeful that the American dream was still achievable.

Halcyon's success brought prosperity, and with prosperity came a desire for culture. This is where Ariel Smith stepped in as the chair of the arts and parks and recreation commission and persuaded the city council to increase funding for the Deer Creek Arboretum and the Playhouse Theater.

Rumors abounded regarding her personal life, even if the facts were clear to everyone—Tom Hayden and Ariel Smith had a child, Abbey. Nothing suspect there. Hayden spent most nights with Ariel and Abbey at a condo he owned on a street behind the official mayor's residence.

Several of the mayor's political supporters argued that these facts revealed to the public, even advertised, could boost the mayor's reelection popularity because he was no deadbeat dad. The other half of the mayor's inner circle feared that a mayoral girlfriend, even one as competent as Ariel Smith, might grate against the grain of the city and its large number of traditionally married voters.

Hayden's inner circle aside, the mayor's chief private counselor was his common-law wife. He said to her, "Our political life would all go down the drain if we admitted giving up our firstborn." Ariel nodded her agreement. During the typical election cycle, the Carver Trust and OmniMedia made sure the words *Hayden*, and *Tom Hayden* were among the most popular Internet search terms in the Valley, triumphing even over the word *sex*, which according to Google is a rare feat.

None of this was complicated or confusing or out of line. City officials and legislators thought of themselves as hardworking public servants with nothing to hide, but there was always something in one's life, professional and private, that could bring public shame, or perhaps even destroy a career if brought into the open. The rise of Dustin Lewis and the death of privacy alarmed many. Denunciations quadrupled and two officers had to be taken off their regular patrol duties to handle the increased workload. Tag Orr made a note in his file that would charm future archive researchers: *Abbey is an open government secret.*

26 THE WHISTLEBLOWER

At first, no one knew Halcyon had an *E. coli* problem, no one suspected the presence of toxic chromium and mercury, as well as arsenic traces. Rumors circulated that tourists were being taken to the hospital but there were no publicly available official reports. OP operatives had classified unwelcome health information as top secret. Tourists were coming down with stomach sickness, twitching, and dehydration. The humorists said it was an overdose of sex. Genital fatigue. But the city was hiding the stats. The bad health numbers were secretly catalogued and kept from the public.

Abbey sensed trouble in the uneasiness shown by her parents. On occasion her mother would appear anxious, sleepless, her father lost in thought, and sometimes abrupt. Though their investment in Halcyon had paid off and showered Abbey with growing-up benefits beyond a mayor's salary, money wasn't what motivated them—the city was the center of their lives.

Dr. Wilkin, a nationally recognized health official, a retired Deer Creek physician and champion of women's reproductive rights, had compiled a critical preliminary report about the sex-surrogate spa industry titled *Poisoned Halcyon Waters*. Mayor Hayden, and much of the Deer Creek business crowd, was losing sleep over it.

Halcyon was a goldmine for the city, a money-churning spa industry framed as a happy village within the city of Deer Creek. Halcyon tripled the city's summer population. It was the go-to place for hip European health tourists, who were attracted by the health-giving reputation of Halcyon's spring-fed spa waters. Tourists also took advantage of the sex-surrogate therapy programs. No one had to use outlawed rhinoceros horn, and prescriptions for Cialis and Viagra were booming. A local bar renamed itself The Four-Hour Erection. The sex surrogates, male and female, were exceptionally beautiful.

But Dr. Wilkin's report was a damning indictment of government ineptitude. The mayor invited legislators to an executive session to discuss Halcyon—reporters and the public were barred from the meeting. Kirstin Powell, the planning manager, had just told those attending that the water could be treated to make it safe. But there was no mention of toxic chromium, mercury, or arsenic traces in the report that she'd ordered.

The mayor shook his head in dismay. "One hundred thousand bucks for his report? We hired these guys?" He wanted to roar, but he lowered his voice. "How the hell are we going to get naturist-oriented health tourists to fly across continents to bathe in 'natural, spring-fed waters' that are *chlorine*-treated for God's sake? Our sex bunnies don't like chlorine in their 'natural' waters. Our water is supposed to be magical. Even miraculous!" He shook his head again. "Chlorine."

"We don't have to tell anyone we're using chlorine," Kirstin Powell said.

The mayor was still shaking his head. "These people can travel anywhere in the world. We tell them the therapeutic quality of our water offers health miracles beyond those at Lourdes."

He wanted to shout. But John Foster had warned him to reign in his hot-button temper—he was alienating staff and councilmembers alike. "This is off the record?" Hayden checked to make sure that the recording button in front of him was pushed to the off position.

"The minutes won't be published," Powell reassured him.

"Hey, Ernst, what do you have to say?" the mayor asked.

Councilman Ernst Riddle put away his iPad. "I don't see a problem. Our *drinking* water is piped in separately. It's pure, it's clean. Let's pitch the positive. The tourist crowd isn't supposed to *drink* the spa water, just bathe in it."

"But there could be cross contamination," someone said.

They looked at the carafe of water and a dozen glasses set out on the conference table. A communal shudder seemed to seize the group.

"If that gets out," Lewis said, "the condo market will dry up." He'd kept a low profile during the meeting because he was secretly recording it and didn't want his voice attached to a smoking-gun sound bite.

"Our streets will fill up with boarded-up houses like in Detroit," Mila Stone, a councilwoman, added.

"The problem isn't going to go away," Hayden said. "We'll have to fess up and get it fixed." There was general agreement that it had to be fixed. They all supported the idea, but couldn't figure how to do it quickly or cheaply and did the usual thing; they kicked the can down the road to deal with it later.

The money flowing into Deer Creek from its health industry drowned out most gadflies and critics. Some who persisted in voicing critical comments could expect an OP officer to drop by to "have a cup of coffee" and explain the disadvantages of being a critic of Halcyon. Most were cowed into silence.

Dr. Wilkin remained an exception. His confidential report to the mayor described a looming long-term catastrophe. The Halcyon industry was built on top of an abandoned auto-battery and chromium-plating manufacturing facility. Officials argued that the toxic mineral traces were negligible and conveniently no official wanted to investigate further. Dr. Wilkin, though, continued his unpaid work, tracking the *E. coli* contamination to a nearby quake-damaged sewage-treatment facility. He was working on a final version of his report.

"Yoshiro will bail on the Annex," Ernst Riddle said.

Yoshiro was the managing partner and lead developer. He was planning to break ground the moment the city council voted on a zoning workaround to get rid of people, like Gayle Loftus, living in the trailer park.

"We need a new ordinance," Lewis said, "to strengthen our secrecy laws."

"I'll take care of it," said Brian Lott. He was the council speaker, and hadn't spoken until now.

"Don't announce any hearings," Riddle warned him.

"We'll criminalize the attempt to release city secrets," Lott said. "It'll work like our ordinance criminalizing annoying behavior. We'll make it illegal to send written or electronic communication if such messages might alarm or annoy public servants."

"The *E. coli* plague has to remain top secret," Powell agreed.

At the next council session the city passed an ordinance criminalizing speech that would "annoy or alarm public servants." Dr. Wilkin wasn't mentioned by name, but the law was aimed at him.

27 CENSORSHIP

As these events unfolded, Tag Orr sorted the information that he had collected. He broke no laws to do his work. After his youthful initiation into politics as a field worker he landed a better-paying job as a federal agent with the firearms and tobacco division, seizing unlawful guns being trafficked along the southern Arizona border. After a few years he returned to his first love, and now he trafficked fear, political fear, fear that flourished best when the fog was thickest. And the fog around Deer Creek—its politics, the city council members, Halcyon zoning that legalized sex surrogacy, officials and government authorities, anonymous political contributors—was dense.

Most "oppo" guys worked for one political party or the other to keep it clean of political conflict. Orr played the field, which made him a charming if amoral partner for some of his employers. Like a lawyer he would take any case if you paid him enough, but his heart embraced what he thought was fair. He was an outsider no matter which side hired him, and extremely good at his work because he operated on the premise that everyone was a liar. His suspicious nature served his clients well.

On a previous visit to Deer Creek he had won the confidence of several sources. In his business, a high-level source was best, but he used whomever he could find, and the clerks and drivers and disgruntled secretaries and ex-girlfriends and angry ex-wives and spurned ex-husbands were often available and talkative—provided they could remain anonymous.

With each source, he gained trust and portrayed himself as knowledgeable even if he wasn't fully informed. In that respect, he was like a reporter working to win the confidence of reluctant sources. It took some bullshit but he got close to several sources, including Richie and Rikki. They told him what was going on with Dr. Wilkin's still unpublished preliminary report. Tag Orr couldn't confirm the illness rumors, and no one would give him a copy of the mysterious *Poisoned Halcyon Waters* report. On his follow-up visit to Deer Creek, he tried several times to reach Rikki, but something must have changed in her life. She didn't return his calls.

RIKKI MET RICHIE AT their favorite Benson hangout. She clasped her hands to stop them from shaking. Once again she was afraid that Lewis was having her followed. She left the bar with Richie and they drove separately, weaving in and out of side streets to escape any pursuers. They parked side by side at the Benson Park, and felt momentarily safe. She got out of her car and sat in the front passenger seat of his car.

"I left a friend who was terrified," Rikki said. "The woman was honest with me and said she'd slept with Lewis."

This didn't surprise Rikki. Apparently Lewis had fallen back into his old pattern by visiting sex workers in Benson. The woman he'd visited was small and childlike.

The woman's boyfriend was an informer and thief, and ran criminal errands for Lewis on the cheap. But something must have gone wrong. The woman suspected that her boyfriend had tried to blackmail Lewis. She received a late-night call and was told to go help her boyfriend. She followed directions and found his corpse under the firs with four shots to the head. The woman did not call the Benson cops and made no public statement, but she was afraid she might be next on someone's kill list.

"She's afraid of Lewis. She said Lewis wanted her boyfriend to 'take care of someone.'"

"Did she mention Dr. Wilkin?"

"No. She was packing when I saw her. She's too scared to stay. She's taken another name and is on her way to Vegas."

This was Rikki's first suspicion that Lewis could be capable of extra-judicial killing. She was undecided about what to do, and then she knew: "I have to warn Dr. Wilkin."

They drove in separate cars and weaving through going-home traffic they arrived at Dr. Wilkin's storefront clinic. His nurse had left and he was closing up.

Rikki and Richie repeated all the hearsay and the fears they surmised, but their anxiety made no impression at all on Dr. Wilkin.

"In a routine month I get two death threats."

"Shouldn't you take precautions?" Rikki asked.

"I do. I vary my route and change my schedule unannounced. But none of that will help me escape the silver bullet that's meant for me. If a man has not discovered something that he will die for, he isn't fit to live." He was quoting Martin Luther King, Jr.

28 URGENT MEETING

Orr picked up a call on his cell. "Can you come and meet us?" Orr didn't recognize the voice and asked, "Immediately?" He was wary. Once he'd been held captive for several hours. Several other times he had been threatened. Nowadays, he always called his wife to tell her where he was going; he told her he loved her, and he asked her to kiss the children for him.

Orr asked, "Who are you?" The connection wavered in and out. Another voice came on. "Miss Grover?" Orr said. Faintly he heard yes. He drove to a modest rambler and Rikki let him in. It was furnished simply and he assumed it was her rented house after she'd moved out of Gayle Loftus's trailer. Richie was sitting in the small living room. He had a shotgun cradled on his lap.

"I'm unarmed," Orr said. "I'm never armed."

They remained silent, looking at each other.

"Please sit down," Rikki said.

Orr took a seat in the heavily cushioned armchair. Rikki's furnishings were tasteful, provided your taste teetered toward romantic magenta lushness lighted by candles.

After a few minutes of discomfort spent waiting for someone to break the silence, Rikki spoke up. "Can you help Dr. Wilkin?" She paused. Richie got up. He had his hand on the shotgun barrel.

"That's not the way to handle a shotgun," Orr said.

Richie snorted and walked out of the room.

"Your boyfriend has no idea how to be intimidating."

"He's not my boyfriend. He's a business partner."

"I hope it's profitable for you."

Rikki smiled. "No one forces me to do anything I don't want to do."

Another silence followed. Richie came back without the shotgun, holding a can of beer. "Listen to her," Richie said. "Lewis and Yoshiro want to get rid of Dr. Wilkin."

Orr tried to figure it out: what Richie knew, what Rikki knew, what they were willing to tell him, and what had to be guessed. Again, no one spoke for a while. Orr thought he could hear the candles burning.

"Lewis told her that," Richie finally said.

"The deputy mayor?"

Richie nodded. "They want to get rid of Wilkin before he goes public with his final report." Rikki affirmed this with a quick tilt of her head.

"Why would Lewis tell you?" Orr asked.

"He let it slip as a joke," Rikki said.

"A joke can be a joke."

"You don't know this town," Richie said. "They have everyone intimidated."

Deer Creek was a small city with a huge police presence—robust surveillance, red-light traffic cameras, license-plate scanners, and a zero-tolerance campaign to criminalize nonviolent social acts disliked by the pious majority, with the exception of the moneymaking activities allowed in Halcyon.

A cultured schizophrenia informed police operations. Chief Clapton saw the hypocrisy and kept his force out of the cultural war. The task of repression was reserved for Lewis's Order Police, and the OP Method. Without so much as pausing to take a deep breath, the OP accommodated the wealthy and the privileged touring Halcyon to enjoy pot and sex in approved surrogacy programs at the health spas, and clamped down harshly on freelance sex workers and pot dealers outside the moneymaking permissive zone. A line item in the police budget called sex work a profit center. What no one knew at this point was that Lewis hated the privileged consumers he served.

In some respects Deer Creek wasn't so much a city with

the usual cosmopolitan cultural and consumer choices but a frightened town snickering at Halcyon as a morally blighted place that was irredeemably and suspiciously attractive.

"I don't like what's going on," Rikki said. She looked toward the ceiling.

"It's like *Chinatown*," Richie said. "Halcyon is the biggest thing that's happened to this city. Yoshiro is pushing the Annex expansion and Lewis is his backup. Dr. Wilkin's final report would destroy Halcyon."

"You have to believe us," Rikki said.

"They can't let the spa contamination news get out," Richie said.

"It's all tied together," she finished.

As Orr saw it, Deer Creek was a mortal battleground. Dr. Wilkin worked on public safety in the best sense of the term; Dustin Lewis worked on repression and prohibition and incarceration. Wilkin and Lewis were natural enemies and Rikki, unexpectedly, was a link between them.

"Yoshiro wants Dr. Wilkin to go *away*," Richie said.

"Wishful thinking isn't murder."

"Can't you go to the FBI?" Rikki asked.

"If it got out that I clocked in with the feds, my career as an opposition researcher would come to a startling and sudden end." Either he worked for government as he had earlier, or he worked for his clients who gave him money to put into his 401(k) plan and the 529 savings plan to send his kids to college. "Go see Chief Clapton. He's the honest cop in town."

Richie looked at Rikki. A signal passed between them. Richie spoke, "Chief Clapton's officers are outgunned and outmaneuvered by the OP. The OPA crowd has elected four legislators." The city was under the siege of feuding police forces. Orr had waded into a morass.

Rikki wrote down her new cell number. Orr wasn't going to take her number, and then she said, "I'm frightened." He took the card. It read, "Puppet Artist."

"Why me?" he asked.

"There's no one left in Deer Creek who can face the truth," she said.

"You want me to be the town's conscience?"

Rikki went silent. Richie, too.

"That's not in my line of work."

"Our town needs you," Richie said.

Orr wasn't supposed to take sides. Lies were often the currency national governments used. But the idea that an entire *local* government establishment was suppressing troubling news that the public had a right to know in order to be informed on ballot issues wasn't something he had previously confronted in his practice. The rumors troubled him. You're supposed to trust your city, your cops, your neighborly officials, and your local planners and regulators to do the best they can do to serve the public. But administrations small and large, officials, cities, counties and the federal government commit gross crimes against the public good by abusing their power as long as they can shield it in secrecy.

"You've got to help us," Rikki repeated.

"I'll see what I can do," Orr said.

29 BAD OPTICS

"The optics don't look good," said the finance director. He was talking to John Foster and the two of them were riding on a bus that Foster had booked to take city officials en masse to the Ice Palace's grand opening. The project had come in a year late and one-hundred percent over budget just as the city was cascading toward bankruptcy. Foster had brought placards, organized student sign-making workshops and hired a filmmaker to shoot and edit a video to highlight the mayor's leadership. He had assembled a swarm of humanity at the grand opening to demonstrate support for Hayden.

Hayden had a lot of competition. OP denunciations were on the rise, and skepticism dominated. People worldwide were losing their faith in government. The Arab Spring was in full swing. Gadhafi had been shot. The Chinese party members were keeping their Nobel Prize winner in prison, for proposing Chinese democracy. Putin was smiling murder and had sinister plans afoot. A secret American court was also busy authorizing wholesale spying on American citizens without their consent. Old autocrats and new bureaucrats and favored plutocrats were shuddering at the audacity of their people wanting open discourse, transparency, and a voice in how things were run. The city of Deer Creek was part of the zeitgeist.

A gust of wind smacked the side of the bus, making it sway. Hayden was on the bus too. He wasn't a habitual doubter but his failure to make the city he loved love him back was eroding his personal life. He asked Ariel if she still loved him. He was proud of the woman next to him. The bus was taking them to Hayden's signature civic achievement, the Deer Creek Sports Arena and Ice Palace.

"I hope the speeches are going to be short," Ariel said.

"We love our own voices," Hayden said.

The bus had two more stops to make and was passing the library pick-up point with its gaggle of would-be passengers, among them their daughter Abbey.

"Not to worry folks," the driver said. "We'll get them on the way back from our next stop."

Ariel noticed something interesting. "Do you think we're attracted to people who look like us?"

"I doubt it. I thought that opposites attract."

Ariel's heart was in turmoil. "My puppet performing

star is standing next to Abbey. She echoes something of Abbey's appearance." Thoughts about Trinity clouded Ariel's mind.

Hayden leaned over to take a look. "Rikki Grover?" He squinted to see out the smoked windows. "Dustin Lewis has been parading her around the office."

Ariel turned away from the window. "We should have kept Trinity. We should keep our promises, even the unspoken and unscripted ones."

"I have a clear conscience. She's probably leading the life of a princess."

"I have a bad feeling."

"Would it have made you feel better to have aborted Trinity?"

The shock of the question frightened her.

"Stop thinking about it," Hayden said. "Move on."

"You're just a politician."

"*Just* a politician? That's an indictment?"

The bus swayed as it exited the library parking lot.

"You're always selling. Selling something," she said.

"City fish before it starts to smell?"

His joke fell flat. He had practiced the get-along, go-along ways of government for so long that it had become instinctual, never saying what first came to his mind, what he thought was fair, but aiming higher or lower depending on what he was negotiating, smoothing his words to accommodate his listeners, expecting, always, to compromise. His flaw, she realized, was that he was too eager to make a sale, too willing to compromise.

They'd become political junkies. They'd invested so much of their lives to run for political office that all other options appeared less attractive. Had it been otherwise, Hayden might have been Ariel's starter marriage that ended in divorce. Not that she would have planned it that way. Or they could have grown and prospered together in a conventional household. You never know.

"How about us getting married?" Hayden asked. They were no longer dependent on Ann Carver's monthly allowance.

"Are you feeling threatened?"

"Like never before. The scavengers are circling."

She could read his thinking. "Our marriage will help your reelection?"

"It could. A church wedding?"

"We've never been apart."

"We could make it official."

She held back.

"You think Gayle will keep our secret?" he asked.

"By my count this is the third time you've brought up the fear that the public won't look kindly on us for abandoning Trinity."

"What was I supposed to do? Be an unpaid intern and a dad? You were in Manhattan going to school, and I was waiting for you in D.C."

"I didn't know what kind of a guy you'd turn out to be."

He looked glum. "How did it turn out?"

"We're not finished yet."

"I was going to stand up to Aunt Carver and marry you anyway."

"Yes, you proposed."

"You said no."

"You took the Carver money."

"So you said no for my sake?"

"You didn't push too hard when I turned you down. I needed someone to bully me then. It all might have gone the other way."

"I've been accused of being pushy, sexist, impolite, and you want me to remain that way?"

"Had you rudely persisted—"

"I do persist. I'm going for gold. I plan to run for governor, use my record as mayor to get elected."

She didn't like his running for higher office. "We could have had a normal life. Two children, two parents. Nothing fancy."

"Did you hear me?"

"Yes, I heard, Governor Hayden."

"You should talk to Gayle Loftus about keeping mum."

"Gayle kept our secret all these years." Ariel's head swam in memories. "Was it you, or was it me who wanted to give up Trinity? We had the income to raise both children."

"It has nothing to do with us now."

"I miss our firstborn."

Ariel had pictured herself as an active and engaged mother, and of course she hadn't been there for Trinity. But she'd seen no way forward at the time. Tommy was charming, well spoken and intelligent, and he came along with his rich family. He owed his career to Ann Carver, who'd never stopped loathing Ariel.

Ariel, according to Ann, had been the poor pick-up prize. She wasn't the old-money, privileged young wife they'd thought the Carver family deserved. She wasn't a celebrity, or a smart academic, or a talented musician—what she wasn't could fill a book. Privately, they said Tom was floating downstream, abandoning his education, bottom fishing and sacrificing his future. They'd never liked her.

"Would you have gone further in life without me?" Ariel asked.

He blew a puff of air. "What's tangling your mind today?" He put his arm around her shoulders. "Come on, sweetheart." They were special together, going back all those years.

"I think I'm even smarter than most of your Carver relatives. The thing-iness of their lives is always on display—the sculpture gardens, the luxury cars, the cruises, the wines, the extra houses, and the Carver plane and helicopter you've used. Your business-minded cousins, they're lawyers and MBAs, they prattle on about government moochers, productivity, return on investment, arbitrage, price, and expensive getaways and summer homes and stocks and derivatives and IPOs and venture capitalists." She searched for the meaning in their lives. "They buy things."

"We're all grateful to our great-grandfather for having been such a successful business bastard."

She saw her good-hearted Tommy, her Braveheart, as an outlier from the Carver clan, moving beyond their conspiracy to rule in favor of elites. "Do you really think that Trinity was adopted into a well-off, educated family?"

"Why should I think otherwise?"

"In my head I hear your aunt's voice every morning. Giving up Trinity was the worst thing I'd done in my life."

She now saw for the first time how chancy and unreliable the natural world is, how good luck and bad luck shamelessly consort with each other, how irreducibly fickle love is—a chance to surrender or conquer, or go berserk. She saw how innocents are often punished and the evildoers rewarded. She saw hard work go unrequited. She saw how easy it was to lose everything, to lose it all at once and forever.

"I'm like Chekhov's Gurov," she said, thinking about *The Lady with the Dog*. "Gurov 'had two lives, an open one, seen and known by all who needed to know it, full of conventional truth and conventional falsehood, exactly the lives of his friends and acquaintances; and another life that went on in secret.'"

Ariel's secret past and the present were hurtling toward a collision.

"Out, out, dark spot. Out, shame," she said.

"Another play you're putting on?"

"Shakespeare, except he said it differently: 'Out, damned spot! Out, I say.'"

She was now a local celebrity, a role model, a former businesswoman, the respected chair of the arts and parks and recreation commission, and the mayor's steady live-in girlfriend. Fessing up, admitting she had a daughter she'd abandoned, no matter how well justified it might have appeared at the time, would poison the respect she commanded. What's more, it would undermine, perhaps even destroy, Tom's bid for higher office.

30 RIBBON CUTTING

The bus made its rounds, collected everyone, and disgorged the passengers en masse at the gala ribbon-cutting event. The political elite, the polished and the powerful, and the everyday Deer Creek officialdom, milled about before heading toward the dais and speaker's platform.

The city's emblem was a hummingbird alighting on a flower. That sentiment aside, a squad of stout and broad-shouldered Order Police dominated the scene. They stood at attention holding their black flags embroidered with blazing silver Os. The first letter stood for Observation, followed by Order, and Obedience. The public, though, had nicknamed them Triple Zeros, angering Lewis. He was dressed for the occasion in his OP blacks. A peaked cap added to his stature, its gold braid sparkling. Rikki was with him. Mayor Hayden and Ariel Smith were ahead of them.

The media crowd had assembled near the TV van. A local reporter had once interviewed Ariel. He described her as a cosmopolitan who had returned to her beloved hometown to start a fashion school for teenagers. Nothing came of the fashion school. The "cosmopolitan" label stuck however, which was all right if you were the nation's first lady, but it wasn't a good thing in a city with a small town mentality, almost like an unwanted tattoo. Ever since then she'd worked at being down-home, wearing fleece and nondescript sweaters bought at T.J. Maxx, but she couldn't hide that she was attractive. The air around her held vitality, a hint of mystery. And she was incapable of saying anything stupid. For this event she'd put away her homespun look, and remained alongside Hayden, every inch on fashionable display in a red ensemble. She saw Rikki and Lewis huddled below the scaffolding that supported the speaker's platform, and overheard them too.

"You'd better stay behind," Lewis said to Rikki.

"All the children and wives and family are up on the dais," Rikki said.

"Let's not go public yet."

"You're ashamed of me?"

"I'm not ready," he said.

"I'm your hideaway girlfriend?"

"Babe."

"You're in it too far to back out," she said.

"You're pretty sharp, aren't you? I'm doing my best to—"

"To keep me hidden. What if I went public?"

"You won't," he said confidently, leaving her behind.

Rikki saw Richie standing in the event staging area and joined him. They sat on a bench under a maple tree for a peekaboo view of the dais. The seats alongside them and the space in front of them were stacked with catering supplies for the gala grand opening. It was as private as Richie could hope for, and he was thrilled to have Rikki to himself. He knew she was a perfectionist, living on the edge of disappointment every day. "Your lover has just publicly spurned you. The dick."

She shrugged. She didn't like it that Kirstin was standing so close to Lewis.

"You can't love that asshole deputy mayor?"

"I don't have to love him. I need him."

"You need *me*."

"I need you?"

"That's right. You should've seen me in action yesterday. I sold more carpet to that Yoshiro guy in one day than I sold in an entire month to a bunch of customers. I'm going to be the biggest carpet merchant this town has ever seen! I've said goodbye to Fox Furniture. I'm going indie. I've got suppliers in my corner. Wood and tile flooring. Trend Carpets, Continental is coming. I've got Mohasco making Mohawk carpets and Alexander Smith carpets, and wool too! Mohasco is going to lend me money if I want to franchise. I've got a big-deal local business broker chasing my ass to partner with him. He thinks I should get into business developing venture stuff."

"My heart is with you."

"Then come with me. We're going to have the ride of a lifetime. We can make a home just for us."

"You're a sweetheart."

He held up his hands as if directing an orchestra. "Rikki and Richie, Rikki and Richie. We're still very young."

"We're young," she said, charmed by his energy.

"You know that it's not the sex between us. I wouldn't care who you fucked for business or pleasure. I'll be there for you."

"That almost sounds like love."

She'd like to experience more of it. She believed love was different from romance. Her observation was neither profound nor new, but it satisfied the empty moment. Everyone should experience love, she thought, even though not everyone does. What most everyone experiences is romance, which is fun and unpredictable. Romance runs wild and is unfaithful to the past. It's the cradle of Valhalla, unruly, all hope and all loss, a sword or a suicidal rope. Romance withstands all interpretation, repeats itself, and is never dull. Love on the other hand can be ordinary and rare at the same time, and if you're lucky it endures after romance dies.

"I'm ready today. You can join me today," Richie said. "We'll do several stores. A chain of them. Even franchising."

"Give me some room. Please let me breathe." She was

distracted by the sight of Kirstin Powell standing behind Lewis on the dais. Abbey was with her parents, smiling, holding balloons by their strings.

Richie withdrew for a while. And then he came back. "You think I'm just fooling around? Big bullshit Richie? Let me tell you, Deer Creek is booming. I never made as much money in my life. The builders and developers are going crazy. And every damn building needs a floor to walk on. Like gravity is in my favor."

"You're adorable," she said.

"I don't see what you see in that dude."

"He's got qualities."

"And I'm just a fucking salesman?"

"Richie!"

"Me an' Willy Loman. Ariel Smith is putting on *Death of a Salesman*. She gave me a bit part I have to study up on. A stupid kid named Biff."

"That's funny."

"What's funny?"

"You don't like to read."

"I'm going rogue on this one. No descriptions, only dialogue." He waited a moment. "This fits my business strategy, brushing shoulders with the people who go to see the plays. The silverhairs, I call them. They can afford to buy carpeting."

She was still focusing on Kirstin. "Lewis is ashamed of me."

"What a dick."

"He's got a heart," she said.

"He's a killer. A strutting bantam killer."

The autocrat in Lewis had a hard edge that attracted her, although she wasn't sure why.

"You and me, you know?" Richie went on. "We can take on the world. You'll be the interior designer. I'll be the sales hustler. We can make them believe in us."

"I don't know formal design."

"I don't either. We'll learn on the job. Come with me and be my partner. You can be yourself. You won't have to hide in public."

"I'm not hiding."

"If you say so."

When she'd started dating Lewis she'd learned to lower her smile. She watched her posture closely, sitting, posing, and walking. She wanted to be confirmed in other people's eyes, and the effort left her suspicious, wary of daggers, knives out to cut her.

"You know what Lewis is afraid of?" Richie asked. "You shouldn't have posted a selfie with you in a fur coat carrying a sign that said, 'Will work for diamonds.'"

"The fur was fake."

"Yeah, but the picture."

"I was protesting the rich getting to do what they want at Halcyon and my girlfriends getting busted."

"Now you're an activist for sex workers?"

"I'm working toward getting some light shed on the subject."

"You won't get far. Not in a town where the OP commander fucks you and wants to arrest anyone who does the same thing. He wants to outlaw male desire. He wants to criminalize human behavior."

Rikki didn't want to criminalize male desire. Boys were attracted to her. Men were attracted to her. That was a good thing, useful in life. Women liked her. She'd drawn fire from the church-based community by putting on a comic puppet show with happy gay parents. She could take the fire and fire back. Bisexual, hetero or gay, she'd never worried about those distinctions.

For his part, Richie adored her. "I don't think sex is all *that* important."

"Don't tell that to my clients."

"You're my touchstone for happiness," Richie said.

"Happiness?" She brushed the floppy hair from his forehead, running her fingers along the solid hairline, and smiled gratefully.

31 TRIPLE ZEROS

Tag Orr stood on the sidelines of the ribbon-cutting ceremony while photographing the local luminaries with a tiny clip-on camera that took a shot every thirty seconds. He had noted in his report that the city bureaucracy was becoming rigid and rule-bound, a study in contrasts and contradictions. Officials insisted that they worked for openness and inclusion in government, but they were systematically limiting access and censoring public information. Hayden was nominally a progressive mayor, but there was nothing in the progressive playbook that took second place to the autocratic playbook when it came to suppressing unwanted questions and hiding embarrassing information.

Deer Creek was far ahead of the nation in another way—perhaps unintentionally, it had become an advanced government lab for exploring the best way to control and suppress human behavior by criminalizing it. Orr noted that the United States has less than five percent of the world's population but jails twenty-five percent of the world's prisoners, more than China, more than Russia, more than Europe.

To be simultaneously the Land of the Free, and jail more citizens than any country on earth had jailed ever before, took some tricky dancing. The Order Police illustrated the progressive steps officials often follow to establish a surveillance police state. First, the loss of civil freedom has to be legal—thus new ordinances rained down upon the city, criminalizing "annoyances" that are part of the democratic package. The distinction between crimes and annoyances soon collapsed in Deer Creek. The city had to build a larger jail to hold all the people charged with annoyances. What was an annoyance—that remained fuzzy, and left up to the OP to decide in each case. Critics of the OP Method were an annoyance. Several reporters were working on computer-assisted research projects to get to the bottom of it.

OP officers strategically placed Wi-Fi sensors throughout town, each the size of a deck of cards and easily concealed. They logged mobile phones entering the interagency district. The sensors automatically logged every move from grocery store to liquor store to church to motel to sex-surrogate center to restaurant to spa. There was enough private information to blackmail anyone, especially if he or she engaged a sex worker and then went to church. Lewis had ordered powerful servers to keep the data in storage forever. Those who understood how the sensors worked and had business in town either used throwaway phones or left their smartphones at a secure place, and retrieved them when they were finished with Deer Creek.

Anonymity, the right to be left alone, the right to be forgotten, that privacy thing that allows a person to drop out of sight and adopt a new identity and start over fresh, was absent in Deer Creek. The Order Police knew who you were—who was whom and what was what—and they wouldn't let you forget it. The OPs imposed total surveillance, and ruled by using informers and denunciations.

What was unusual about Lewis's anti-privacy campaign was the argument he made in favor of it. He said privacy belonged to the government. Privacy was so precious that it had to be regulated. Lewis had gotten ahead of the national privacy debate. Each citizen had to apply to the OP to secure a morsel of privacy, and requests were routinely denied because public safety always trumped individual privacy.

He was riding an authoritarian groundswell.

The OP operatives showed up at the mall regularly to display their uniforms and weapons, and distribute silver triple-O lapel pins that the officers wore on their black uniforms. Prominent Deer Creek residents declared their support for the triple Os by wearing the lapel pins. Higher officials bought pins made out of gold. A jeweler could add diamonds for those who could afford them.

Businesses, too, started to display the triple Os next to the "support your police" decals. Before anyone knew what was happening the symbol had spread like a fast-moving flu. Cars had it on license-plate holders and many homes had a large bronze triple-O rising on a post near the front door or a smaller triple-O next to the doorbell or doorknocker. It got so that officials expected to see the triple-O symbol before giving you service. If you couldn't show them your triple-O pin, and you needed help at a city office, the odds were good that you'd have to wait longer than those who were wearing a triple-O pin. The symbol became so entrenched that the city council passed a resolution declaring that Deer Creek supported triple-O principles.

A secret administrator chosen from among high-ranking police officials administered the rules governing these principles. The rules and the principles were too secret to reveal because they might expose the OP's capabilities; thus the rules had to be kept secret to keep them out of a potential enemy's hands. In fact, the triple-O principles were never fully described, transcribed or published. For one thing they were complex, like the tax code, consisting of sections and paragraphs and subsections, and most non-lawyers couldn't decipher them accurately. Also, the rules changed often, and no one wanted to be identified with a discredited rule. Nevertheless, to do business in the city, people had to sign a statement that they supported triple-O principles.

The principles were considered inflexible, but their

application varied. One example that escaped OmniMedia censorship and made it into the local news was called "the colonoscopy arrest."

The Order Police stopped a nervous man outside Halcyon because they suspected him of drug dealing. (Actually he had visited a sex worker.) They strip-searched him and didn't find what they were looking for, but he looked so nervous that they knew in their hearts that he was hiding drugs. They had to search the only place left to search, his anus. They handcuffed him naked to a chair. The smell was awful at the end of ten hours, but still no evidence. The Order Police knew in their hearts that he was in possession of drugs. Two burly OP officers inserted an enema suppository. This procedure dehydrated the suspect and left another mess. Then they drove him to the local Catholic hospital where a doctor performed a colonoscopy. Again, no evidence was found.

They had to release him. They told him he hadn't been arrested, only detained for his own safety—the OP had changed its story and said that he was a mule who could have swallowed a condom packed with drugs that might have burst and killed him. They had detained him for his own good. The hospital billed the man for the colonoscopy. An OP sergeant asked to comment said that the matter was an internal one, and that he couldn't comment, but then he went on to comment anyway: "Just because there was no evidence doesn't mean that he isn't guilty." That was one of the most powerful and frequently applied unpublished triple-O principles: everyone was guilty until proven innocent.

Orr watched the ribbon cutting. His tie-clip camera continued taking pictures. He overheard the mayor asking Dustin Lewis to meet him in his office. At the end of the speechifying, most of the gathered rushed to a buffet table set out for the occasion. Orr went to City Hall instead.

32 THUNDERSTRUCK

Dustin Lewis was in his office at City Hall, his anger festering as he waited for the mayor to call him to a meeting with Police Chief Clapton. He switched on the video and revved up AC/DC's "Thunderstruck" extremely loud. City Hall, although painted white, was closer to a doghouse than to the White House. The offices were small and cramped. Hayden couldn't concentrate half the time he was there for all the interruptions pounding on his skull.

Thunderstruck, thunderstruck, yeah, yeah, yeah.

"Turn the fuckin' thing down!" Hayden shouted.

Lewis silenced AC/DC and walked the hallway connecting his office to the mayor's. He was still wearing his black uniform. He stopped in front of the mayor's oval desk.

"Yeah, yeah, yeah, thunderstruck," the mayor muttered to himself.

"I want it," Lewis demanded.

The mayor knew immediately what Lewis wanted. "You want to fuck away three hundred thousand dollars on a BearCat while the city is going broke?"

Lewis was eager to buy a Lenco armored personnel carrier that was being marketed to small cities as a "rescue vehicle." He kept pacing. "I want it."

"Stop menacing the crap out of my fuckin' floor."

"It's a public-safety issue."

"For God's sake, sit down," the mayor said.

Lewis sat. He clenched his fists. His mind was doing cartwheels and his face flooded with passion. "This isn't about me."

Hayden's once docile deputy mayor had become difficult. Supported by the thousands of voters who'd joined the OPA Lewis had become an independent power, introducing new surveillance laws, shoveling them past the city council with a veto-proof majority and dumping the new ordinances on obedient citizens as "public-safety" laws.

The OP was having a banner year arresting people for noisemaking, open beer container violations, marijuana possession, jaywalking and disorderly conduct, and especially for disturbance of the peace. The last could be anything—even photographing cops on duty, or photographing an ambulance taking sick tourists to the hospital as Rikki had done, or showing authority a raised finger, albeit a middle finger. The jail budget was busted, overtime was skyrocketing. Concilmembers kept adding new laws to criminalize behavior.

Police Chief Clapton came in and joined the meeting. He was in his sixties, a barrel-chested bulldog with a neck size of seventeen inches. He was the patriarch of the local police agencies. "We can now gas people in their own buildings," he announced, startling Hayden.

Lewis was restless. He and Clapton loathed each other.

Clapton went on, "We can kill all the tourists en masse."

Hayden got it. He smiled. Clapton was trying to seduce him with irony. His police chief was a traditional lawman, and Lewis the rogue warrior. "Shock and awe," Hayden said, unable to control his wit.

"Get off my case," Lewis said. "The M113A1 Army tracked vehicle I got us is sitting in your police pound *unused*."

Clapton nodded in agreement. "Also the mine-resistant, ambush-protected MRAP truck that comes with a turret-mounted, belt-fed .50-caliber machine gun that can shoot through buildings."

"You're degrading our capabilities," Lewis said. "We've got to be prepared. I've got us M79 grenade launchers. I've got us flash-bang grenades. I've got us M16s and those fifteen-hundred-dollar tactical vests. All of it for free from the military through the Law Enforcement Support Office. Free. All of it free. Not a penny spent from the city budget." Silence, and then, "Chief, can't you see the logic of free? You got the gear for free."

"Lewis, you're going to wear me out before I retire," Clapton said.

"None too soon."

"Come on, guys. We've got potholes in the street we can't fix because we don't have the money. We need three hundred thousand for a fire truck! Lewis, you want a new police toy?" Hayden lowered his voice. "What are we going to do with it? Conquer lost territories? The council is bitching about patching up the old fire truck that's costing us more to repair every year."

"A grant from the Department of Homeland Security will buy us our BearCat."

"God bless the federal government," Hayden said. "God bless our stupid taxpayers."

"Rikki put in a grant to the DHS."

"I told you to fire her."

"I gave her notice."

"What? A fuckin' year's notice?"

"She's in an authorized planning department slot."

Hayden gave his lean deputy an icy glance. "I ordered a hiring freeze. I want her *off* the city payroll."

Clapton raised a hand to get some attention. "Did you hear the latest? Lewis wants to take over the regular police force too."

"It's not going to happen on my watch," Hayden said. "Too many things have gone wrong already."

"Lewis has a consultant looking into new uniforms. He

wants our community police to have a menacing look. Full battle dress like his OP guys. He's gone behind my back to get bids to repaint our police vehicles with a menacing cross-hatched pattern."

"We're an elite organization," Lewis said. "We're tough. We want to look powerful. We're expected to be aggressive."

The chief kept his hands on his knees. "We're supposed to be a democracy, not a fascist state. My job is community policing, not community suppression. We don't have any terrorism here."

"We've got Dr. Wilkin."

This was the first mention of Dr. Wilkin as a domestic terrorist.

"You've got to take control, you've got to be in control," Lewis said. "What have you done about the Occupy Benson Park sit-in? Have you stopped the teachers from striking? We're in the forefront of civil society. We rule by law but democracy will be the ruin of it. The chattering voices. The endless arguments. Everyone his or her own judge. We can't have it. We can't permit it. We use repression to keep our city safe, our people safe. Freedom wants to be free from crime, from confusion. I've a vision, a singular and powerful vision that will make people choose obedience. I want to convince everyone it's in his or her own best interest to obey us. We need a great police force to make it work, to build a great city. A fresh, vibrant, clean city. It would last a thousand years. OP rules! A city with only the best people living here."

The chief got up to leave. Hayden asked him to wait. Clapton hesitated. "When one of my guys starts talking about seeing visions I tell them to go check in with their mental health practitioner."

"Bull! Repression works. I want to make sure there's no place to hide. Repression is our friend. You've got to have an open mind on this, Chief."

"Open mind?"

"A mind is like a parachute. It doesn't work until it's open," Lewis said.

"Your mind is so open that your brains are spilling out."

"Come on, guys, cut it out," Hayden said. "We need to plan our response to Dr. Wilkin's report. He wants a full show with all the councilmembers and city officials present. I want a confidential meeting arranged out of town."

"I'll get on it," Lewis said. The meeting broke up.

33 CRISES LOOMING

The office workers who didn't attend the Ice Palace gala had lowered their guard, which was why the public-records clerk was cooperative with Tag Orr, which was why Orr had the most productive afternoon since his arrival in Deer Creek.

Back at his motel room he studied photocopies of council meeting minutes. There was nothing in the minutes to suggest that a Deer Creek crisis was looming. Unanimous votes approved street improvements and traffic revisions. Friendly public resolutions and anodyne announcements touted local pride, community openness, goodwill, grants, gifts, business openings and letters of support. From all appearances the city was a good-news city.

Orr's sources told him that some legislators and citizens were opposed to Hayden's initiatives, and Hayden realized that the best way to keep them off balance was to keep them in the dark about his priorities and intentions.

Hayden's drift from openness to secrecy could have been predicted, meandering from "just get the facts right and make a good decision" to "make a deal with intransigent political enemies" and finally to "fuck them, I'll do what I want." He couldn't, though, endure the prime-time scrutiny and the endless deflating pinpricks that officials had to either accept or ignore. Transparency became murky in his administration and ended up being opaque, and finally when the water contamination threat came around, obfuscation took center stage.

Policy work had turned out to be tougher than Hayden had expected. That's when he surrounded himself with loyalists who joined his raft to power. One of the first to board the raft, and the most loyal in the beginning, even zealous, was Dustin Lewis. After those early, heady days, weariness set in. Hayden woke each morning thinking, *Et tu, Brute?* The mayor's enemies were rooting around his undead body to see what they could salvage. In the mayor's view, his enemies now included Dr. Wilkin. The doctor said that he loved Deer Creek and wanted to save it from its politicians. Hayden, like every city official, believed Dr. Wilkin was a traitor.

Orr recalled a civics lesson from high school. His teacher had assigned *On Civil Disobedience* by Henry David Thoreau, originally published as *Resistance to Civil Government*. She said everyone has a duty to speak up against power when he or she senses something is wrong that needs to be made right. Officialdom was running amuck in Deer Creek. It was the government vs. the people, and the government was winning.

Orr mulled it over. America had been invented for adventurers and dreamers, a land open to serial rebirths made possible by abandoned pasts. You could change and you could start over. But that too was changing. Government officials of every rank and at every level were pushing for the end of privacy for every citizen, claiming that the right to be left alone, the right to be forgotten, was too old-fashioned to contemplate in the modern world of high-tech surveillance.

He put his pen down, leaned back in the chair, and seized by a thought, he picked up the pen again. "Democracy will never keep citizens safe from tyrants," he wrote. "The tyrants are you and me, and our neighbors."

34 FRIENDSHIP

As for Rikki and Abbey, their friendship thrived with a glowing new intensity, strange and wonderful, and neither of the two sisters could fathom it. They felt better when they were together; the air was sweeter, the sounds more mellow, the flowers more vivid. The passage of time felt insignificant, eternally recurring.

"You think you have angels watching out for you," Rikki said.

"Why shouldn't I believe in angels?" Abbey asked.

"You grew up so protected that you don't know how to recognize danger. I couldn't have survived that way, and my survival was always at stake."

"Fear is stupid," Abbey said.

"Fear is your friend."

"Not *my* friend. I'm never going to die," Abbey said. "I

don't want to." She felt her body tingling, a special alertness, an eagerness, as if moving toward something exciting, toward something special.

During the ice-skating season they went to the rink every week. Abbey held her rented ice skates by their long laces, the blades glistening. Rikki, being the taller of the two, would spot a place for them to sit and put on their skates. She kneeled to loosen the laces of Abbey's skates and pull the tongue out of the boot and widen the ankle leather to let Abbey's foot slip into each skate. Then she smoothed the woolen socks and guided each small foot into the boot leather that would keep Abbey's ankles from twisting. She felt responsible for doing it right. Her attention was such that she hardly noticed her own kneeling position.

Often they skated in silence except for the scraping noise of the blades on the ice, side by side, going round and round, leaning into the middle, a breath away from each other, Abbey's red cheeks glowing. Their time passed in quickening ripples, smaller and smaller, gone all too soon.

On this occasion, Rikki drove Abbey home, parked, and saw the mayor's expensive car in the driveway. "How come I never see you in it?"

Abbey was too young to drive. That aside, she said, "I don't like to be stared at."

"And you want to be a model or actress?"

"Yeah, but that's different, totally, being stared at and being an actress people want to see." Abbey got out of the car and went to the driver's side. They locked their Janus coins and hugged and then Rikki drove away.

35 HOME RULES

Ariel Smith was attending a late-night commissioners' meeting. The mayor was at home reading a report. Abbey shrugged off her jacket. The print on her shirt said, "Money Sucks." The mayor, amused, read it out loud.

"Oh, Dad."

"Was that your boyfriend who dropped you off?"

Abbey wanted to signal her grown-up status. "What if it was?" She hummed as if distracted, caught between a wish to be taken seriously, and a wish to remain truthful.

"I hope your mother has talked to you about girly things."

"I don't *do* anything. I don't plan on *doing* anything."

"We don't want you hurt."

She tried to sound indifferent. "I'm not going to get hurt." She lowered her chin. Her hair swung forward and partially hid her face. The boys at her private school carried expectations on their shoulders like epaulets, and Abbey was wary of them. The boy from Benson was nice but also silly and sometimes mean. Another boy, Jason, she liked more. He had a tender eagerness, a tense energy she hadn't expected in boys. It made her heart jumpy. But she wasn't ready for a special boy in her life, though if she had been ready she would've liked Jason more than she liked the other boys.

The clock in the living room chimed on the hour.

"How come you guys never married?"

"It didn't turn out so bad for you, did it?"

She inclined her head, defensively waiting. "Mom didn't want to marry you? It's been nineteen years now that you guys have been together."

"That's right."

"Can't you make up your minds to commit?"

"Marriage is not the only way to make a commitment."

"I won't be hurt by it."

He gave Abbey a look. "Hurt comes in several packages, some of them quite young and attractive."

"Yeah, whatever." She had accused her parents of hovering over her, but she wasn't complaining, not too much. Her parents had dutifully gone to PTA meetings and school events and teacher conferences and had even quarreled with the principal when he refused to assign Abbey to a teacher widely acknowledged to be superior. They cared. They watched. They protected her.

Still, she would've liked to have a stage mother, if not exactly one who hovered over her, then one who was crazy about acting, or a father who was a famous producer, someone who could guarantee her a high-level position in the profession. But then she thought about Rikki and saw how narrow her choices had been, and she'd managed okay anyway.

"May I invite Rikki home?"

"Rikki Grover?"

"She's dating—"

"I know."

"She's my best friend."

Hayden turned the page noisily. "Isn't she too old for you?"

"I'm not a child anymore."

"Your mom is thinking about sending you to a school in Seattle."

"Because you don't like my friend?"

He was reading *Poisoned Halcyon Waters*.

She waited. "Dad, can you look at me?"

He hadn't yet learned that Rikki was his own daughter. "You'll have to talk to your mother about that."

Part Four

THE CONFLICT

36 CITY BORDERS

Tag Orr had won a small victory in a dispute with a city clerk that day, and the moment still gave him pleasure. "Public records," he had said. "Your job is to provide citizens with the public records they request. It's not part of your job to ask me *why* I want to see the records."

He waited for the inevitable eye rolling and didn't respond when it came. The Freedom of Information Act was a terrific tool, but it often meant months, even years, of delay because at least a third of the time government agencies refused requests on one pretext or another. Orr had to repeatedly go to court to force local governments to follow the law, but he needed information that day. The clerk handed him the tax records on the Halcyon project and the city council voting records.

His Halcyon assignment was straightforward—report on every person involved in developing Halcyon, a huge public and private redevelopment project that had altered Deer Creek's shape and made private fortunes sparkle.

He wanted to know who was kissing whose ass and how much kissing was going on. Deer Creek didn't have K Street lobbyists, but it had plenty of local lobbyists, although they didn't see themselves as such. They saw themselves as church ministers, as businesspeople, developers, as community-college educators; they were retirees, managers, lawyers, and civil servants—stakeholders, as they've often been called, voters with a point of view of how best to channel public tax monies into profitable private benefit. The regular jobholder, mortgage payer, citizens who used to be called the working stiffs, they were nowhere in sight, yet elected officials claimed to speak for them.

Orr kept working for his unknown client. Another clerk was more helpful than the first. She worked quickly to hand him what he asked for. He photocopied a batch of land transaction documents involving the payday king Yoshiro. Hayden and Yoshiro were from the highest economic class in Deer Creek. Yoshiro on account of his entrepreneurial success. Hayden on account of his family's wealth. They should have been natural colleagues sailing smoothly on the bow of money, but they were enemies. It had started with the banning of Yoshiro's dog, Penny, from Halcyon.

Yoshiro loved his salt-and-pepper miniature schnauzer,

but the mayor hated dogs messing city sidewalks even if people were obliged to pick up after them. When no one was paying much attention, Hayden backed Speaker Lott in a blizzard of clean-up-this-city ordinances, one of which outlawed dogs in Halcyon.

Yoshiro was incensed. His favorite saying was "It's just me and cash and my Penny." He was forced to rent his new house in Halcyon to tourists because he couldn't keep Penny on the premises. He nursed his grievance, waiting for the right moment to strike at Hayden.

Orr folded the photocopied documents into a file. He was ready to leave.

"Mr. Orr," the friendly clerk said. He liked her. She was among the many competent civil servants working for the city. "You've had a difficult time arranging meetings with the staff?"

"That's an understatement."

No matter how clean Orr's practice, city employees, local pols and the public at large assumed he was looking for dirt. And though Orr denied it vehemently and often, they were right.

"You can reach some of them off-duty."

"I'd like to. But when they see me coming, they run."

"There's an informal out-of-towner for city officials. The *Flying Dolphin* sailing out of Port Angeles. A fishing trip and stopover at Kalaloch Lodge."

He understood the gift she'd just given him. They smiled

at each other. He thanked her and left. As soon as he got outside he called a booking agent and discovered that the premium captain's suites were always available to high-paying clients even though a good portion of the *Flying Dolphin* had been chartered for a private event. He paid with a credit card. The booking agent e-mailed the itinerary—three days, two nights.

Orr was gambling that something worthwhile would come of it, but it was like him to take a gamble even though he suspected he'd just wasted his client's money.

He checked his watch. Almost time for his meeting.

As instructed, he drove to the Halcyon headquarters and parked in the nearly empty lot. A few minutes later, a sleek, black Mercedes parked next to him. An Asian man was behind the wheel. He rolled down his window and beckoned for Orr to get out and approach the Mercedes.

Orr didn't leave his car.

"I'm Yoshiro," the man said. Penny was in the passenger side seat.

The man was rich, successful, smiling and vain. He had a seat on the local bank board and owned and operated an empire of last-hope payday companies. He was also the managing partner and lead investor in the Halcyon Annex revitalization project. He stepped out of his car. He was medium height and had iron cheeks, a firm chin and eyes that could bludgeon you. He strode over and extended his hand through Orr's opened window.

"What can I do for you?" Orr asked.

"I heard you do dirt."

"You heard wrong."

Orr wasn't brawny, few things scared him and nothing could surprise him, but he felt a chill. Yoshiro paused. Maybe he was deciding whether Orr was too stupid to have this conversation. Orr saw a black holster clipped to Yoshiro's belt.

"Who do you work for?" Yoshiro demanded.

"I work for nobody."

Yoshiro took the answer as a slight. But in a way Orr's remark was true. That aside, he didn't want to come off like a smartass. "My client wants to remain anonymous."

"What's your fee?" Yoshiro asked.

"I work for one client at a time."

Orr never left a fact unchecked and never sat with his back to a window. He always went to a meeting prepared to meet the unexpected.

Yoshiro hesitated. His shirt was crisp. "I pay better." Another pause. An aircraft flew overhead, the noise faded. Yoshiro bent closer. "A quarter of a million dollars?"

The amount caught Orr's attention. "For what?"

"Cash."

Deer Creek liked doing business in cash, Orr noted—always a signal for caution. "What are you saying?"

"You take care of him." The pause was much longer.

"Who?"

"Dr. Wilkin."

"Take care of him?"

"Yes." The eyes were steady. "If our spas are poisoned it would kill us."

The language was ambiguous. Orr wasn't sure if he had just been offered a quarter-million-dollar contract to murder a man. Maybe his imagination was overworked. "You've got the wrong man. My job is to uncover things not make them disappear."

Yoshiro made a gesture that looked like a salute. "Call me when you run out of money." He returned to his car.

Orr went back to his motel room. He was the father of two, happily married, and he missed his kids when the job took him far from home. He called his wife and felt better.

37 THE SILVER HEIRLOOM

The following day Gayle Loftus picked up a call from Yoshiro. "I want you out, out, out," he said, not raising his voice.

Even with Rikki's help Gayle had been unable to catch up, because Yoshiro, in accordance with the late payment penalty clause, demanded full payment of the balance. "Can't you wait?" Gayle asked.

"I'm not in the low-income housing business," Yoshiro answered. His Halcyon Annex penthouse condos were presold for prices above a million dollars. "I want you out, period." He often said "period" to emphasize his demands.

He had several nicknames, "Yoshi" and "Mr. Q" for "Quiet Man," and several that were unprintable. In addition to his Halcyon real estate ventures he operated stores under the names BuyPawn, Mr. K's Easy Credit and Payday

King—all of the companies advertised to the financially disadvantaged: "Broke? Poor Credit? Divorce? Bankruptcy? Bad credit? No credit? 100% credit approval guaranteed. Shop with confidence at Mr. K's Zero-Down Specialists, the Payday Kings! No credit check required."

The ruinous payday-lending rates his companies applied to loans would have shamed a thief. The profits from his startlingly profitable operations, pawning and lending, had bought him several houses, the Halcyon Annex project, and gourmet restaurant food for Penny. In ordinary circumstances he wouldn't have called Loftus, leaving the ugly task to one of his collection specialists, but her refusal to move had caused an extremely costly delay. She'd roused the state to intercede on her behalf, with a homestead claim that had no chance of prevailing in court, but in the meantime Halcyon Annex construction had come to a dead stop until the city could finalize the eviction process.

"Are you still on the line?" Yoshiro demanded.

"You wouldn't do this to your mother," she said.

"You're not my mother."

Tribal instincts ran deep under Yoshiro's skin. His grandparents, U.S. citizens, had been deprived of property and liberty, and though innocent, they were imprisoned in an interment camp in Idaho during World War II. The racist injustice burned in his memory. He had no mercy for anyone.

"It's only a trailer, on a rented lot," he said.

"It's my home."

"Get another home."

She stifled a cry. Yoshiro hung up.

Her trailer was warm that morning. There was no condensation on the walls and by nine the sun had risen high enough above the trailer hedge to light the geranium pots she kept in front of her entry. She remained the faithful unpaid supervisor of the arboretum volunteers.

The trailer park was part of the rezoned Halcyon Annex revitalization area. Yoshiro had parked four bulldozers in front of her manufactured house, as trailers were now described. The bulldozers' plows were threateningly raised, and several backhoes reached over a flimsy fence with their claw-like arms.

As one of the last holdouts she insisted on showing up at the city council meetings and playing on councilmembers' emotions to prevent the city from dispossessing her. Many townspeople defended Yoshiro. The law was the law, they said, a contract was a contract, and Yoshiro was a much-needed last-resort lender. He operated in a badly regulated business zone where the greedy trolled and the naïve and disadvantaged always got slaughtered—paying legal interest rates as high as three hundred percent.

Gayle held a coffee mug to warm her fingers. She was unsophisticated in business matters and thought that if she got caught up on her trailer payments Yoshiro would stop intimidating her. She didn't realize that he wanted her out even if she paid up.

She made an inventory of the items she owned that she could hock at BuyPawn to make her balloon payment to Yoshiro. The irony of having to sell or pawn something with a Yoshiro company to pay off a Yoshiro loan didn't resonate deeply. She was without malice or anger and believed that love won all battles. In the back of her mind, she understood that the little people always paid more and at higher interest rates than the big people in town. She accepted her fate, knowing that she would be rewarded in heaven because she had no camel to push through the eye of a needle.

Her collection of ceramic frogs could bring in some cash. She had a couple of good-looking vases and some silver she never used. Then her eyes settled on the engraved silver box, the size of a large cigar box, the most special thing in her collection. She picked it up and raised the lid. The commemorative baby footprints and Ariel's grateful note inscribed made the box the last exquisite thing Gayle owned. There was no getting around having to sell it or pawn it to pay Yoshiro. Her furniture was derelict, her car on its last legs. Neither furniture nor household goods nor her car was worth anything as collateral. Gayle took a cloth and polished the silver box—she would have to think about it.

38 THE SIEGE

After leaving the mayor's office, Lewis got to work organizing operation "Kalaloch Express." He chartered a bus to take top-level officials to the coast. The long distance from Deer Creek was important—it would keep nosy Deer Creek reporters and bloggers away. The conference was so secret that aside from the official word-of-mouth cover story to explain city officials' absence—the trip was a much-needed respite, a "working vacation"—nothing written or digital existed, no e-mails or letters, no recorded messages, no videoconferencing.

The main subject—what to do with Dr. Wilkin—wasn't mentioned at all. Lewis intended to handle that outside of official and public channels. When the finance director raised questions, the ever-competent deputy mayor said he was arranging the secret conference to tackle a "publicity" problem.

He had passed the travel arrangements on to a list of attendees. Most would travel in the official *Kalaloch Express* bus, but a few wanted to make separate travel arrangements. Among them were Police Chief Clapton and the mayor, who'd hop a flight on the OmniMedia helicopter.

Lewis expected an invitation to join them. Privately, though, he hated Hayden's family privileges. It wasn't just envy—it was visceral hate.

Lewis had barely been able to afford state college, let alone the elite universities. Working full-time, he paid his own way, no scholarships, no grants, no freebies, attending at nights, but unlike the typical success story, looking back with pride and nostalgia at the challenges he'd overcome, he was deeply marred by a class-conscious dislike for the rich kids attending the university—girls and boys alike, the "spoiled children of the privileged" who grow up to ride their inherited chariots. This hatred welled up in Lewis, a primordial wish to eviscerate and strangle his enemies.

He paid lip service to public-private cooperation, government and business working together. Secretly he detested the private business sector and the silver-spoon crowd who'd risen to prominence on the divine right of inherited money. He yammered on about his disjointed social theories to Rikki, his ever-captive audience. The self-made man was a myth, he said. The wealthy progeny always started dozens of steps higher on any ladder they wanted to climb. He hated their yachts. He hated their sixty-thousand-dollar-a-month Manhattan apartment rentals; he hated their private jets, their billion-dollar sports teams; their Lamborghinis and Ferraris, their island getaways and their Paris pied-à-terres, their phony celebrity-serving publicity-seeking charities, their private trusts, their big-name art collections, their fashionable vacation treks, their five-thousand-dollar blouses and suits, and eighty-thousand-dollar sculpted marble bathtubs.

He hated their designers, their high fashion, and their architects. He hated the Carvers and their silver-spoon off-spring, Hayden and Foster. He hated their nepotism. He'd lock them all up. The whole damned generation of them. Freight cars full of them, trust-fund babies hauled from their million-dollar digs.

In a small and unheralded way he'd already started on his trip of vengeance. On his orders whenever the OPs caught any of the rich kids for a minor infraction there were no warnings or tickets issued. The offender had to be hand-cuffed and booked, fingerprinted and mug shot, and if room was available, then held in jail overnight. He was especially harsh with marijuana smokers. He dreamed of a new law that would allow him to keep prisoners in preventive detention for months, maybe even years. The same minor infraction would get a ticket or a warning in other cases. Equal protection under the law was novelty in Deer Creek.

He had a secret plan, a thousand-year plan, a project that would endure. In his mind Deer Creek was a domino, and he was standing tall and ready to push it over. He would mobilize youth and pay them handsomely by requisitioning from the private sector whatever was needed to pay his private army to get the job done—let the rich bastards holler.

He would outlaw secret ballots. He would enforce strict rationing and suppress all dissent and demand absolute loyalty. He would rule by fiat. There would be more parades, gala events and stadium-sized displays of leadership. His propaganda chief would launch a siege on mental complacency. Lewis expected pushback, even revolts. His Order Police would put down the revolts, put people behind barbed wire. He'd march shoulder to shoulder with OPA legions, first in Deer Creek, on to Benson, and then the county, and the state too. The other cities and counties and states would follow his leadership.

He was intimate with the language of messianic conquest. Most of the local titans supported him. They donated to his leadership PAC; they supported his Order Police. But the rich were also at fault, the rich were the curse, bleeding the country, sending their money oversees. Doublethink was a powerful source of Lewis's energy. His self-delusions aside, he had the mind of a man who couldn't invent anything new, and was possessed by a need to diminish those who could. He advertised one thing and wanted to do something else.

Lewis was running a siege, a class war, a domestic war without borders—his enemy everyone, everywhere. A number of the storied rich visited Halcyon and kept Lewis's hate fully inspired. Hayden was personally modest and nowhere near the ultra-consuming rich, but he was closer and easier to hate, and Lewis hated him, too.

39 THE BASEBALL BAT

It was a Saturday. Lewis tracked Rikki's phone using the police Wi-Fi sensors and showed up announced to see her at the arboretum barn, which was warm and smelled of potting soil.

The A-frame ceiling had an electric hoist to help move pallets and bales. The waist-high tables made potting easier. Rikki was so busy that she didn't notice Lewis coming up behind her. He nuzzled her neck and told her how beautiful she was. She resisted.

"Babe, don't be so angry—"

"You won't marry me."

"I didn't say that. Or maybe I said the wrong thing."

"But that's what you mean."

"Babe—"

She threw some potting soil into a pot and yanked one

of the shoots she intended to plant. The gossip had been making the rounds that they were an item together and she didn't mind it. "Ha," she said, sarcastic. "My warrior."

"You're reckless."

"Yeah, yeah. I'm your sneaky pleasure."

"Babe," he pleaded. "Don't fight me."

"Babe, babe, nothing."

"I'll take you to the drive-in tonight."

"Yeah, so no one will see us together."

She relented. They went to buy takeout, and then went to the drive-in. The theater was the last of the drive-ins in the Three Rivers Valley, a wedge chopped out of the woods and bordered on one side by pastureland. Prayer meetings were held on Sundays, and a flea market operated during the weekdays. That evening they were in an Audi A6. He gave her the keys. "I leased it for you," he said. She said thank you, unsatisfied by his grand gesture.

"Did you have my girlfriend's boyfriend killed?"

"You're impossible. Always fighting. Being unreasonable. Babe, come on—"

"You're hunting to get Dr. Wilkin?"

"Don't mess with me."

"I know what's going on."

"You don't know anything," Lewis said. "I'll make sure you stay out of it too." But then he changed his mind and asked her to encourage Dr. Wilkin to come to the out-of-town conference Lewis was organizing.

"Why me?" Rikki asked.

"He'll listen to you."

Popcorn was scattered on the seat.

Prickly and witty and sharp, she'd grown up terrified of authority, afraid of social workers that could break up her foster home and send her packing, cops who could shoot Mr. Clark legally, prosecutors who could get a judge to jail her.

Authorities were the rule-makers and a source of trouble, arrests, citations, warnings, tickets, fines and summonses. Authorities carried guns and now, in Deer Creek, they rode in fourteen-foot-high armored military vehicles that hauled people off to jail for protective detention and coffee chats, and none of this made her feel good. But with Lewis next to her, authority seemed unthreatening, common, banal, and at times even pleasurable.

"You want the car or not?" he asked.

She accepted. He criticized the coming attraction for a movie that dealt with lesbian lovers. "If I had it my way I'd ban degenerate art."

"You'd jail my friends?"

"I'm a straight-up guy."

Rikki pushed on. "I cracked a straight-up guy's head wide open." She aimed to unsettle his instinct to condemn what he didn't understand. Lewis stopped munching and brushed away the popcorn clinging to his jeans. She told him about Stux.

"Stux?" Lewis crumpled the empty bag of popcorn. "I used to work with that guy. He was on the auxiliary police force forever. He wanted to get on with the regulars. An amateur. It doesn't surprise me that he got whacked with a bat." His failure to condemn her took the sting out of her anger.

"The bat?" she said. "Is it still in your evidence room? My fingerprints are on it."

He understood her anxious tone. "I'll fix that."

After the movie Lewis drove Rikki to the evidence room. The officer on duty saluted and left them alone. Lewis located the Stux bat. The blood had dried, and the once-bright scratches were weathered. They left by a back door and he drove her back to her house, where he handed her the bat.

"What should I do with it?" she asked.

"You've got a fireplace, right?"

He crumpled a newspaper, got some wood chips and logs and set a match to the works to get a blaze going. They watched the bat burn and then spent the night together. In the morning Lewis asked, "When is the next time I'm going to see you?"

"I'm looking for work." The city had terminated her.

"You can be an assistant manager at Yoshiro's BuyPawn."

"How much is he paying?"

Lewis told her.

"That's four times what I could expect."

"That's because he owes me."

As Orr noted in his report, Lewis hated the privileged private sector, but he milked them too, and didn't see his toadying up to Yoshiro as troubling. Orr concluded the Lewis portion of the report: *Lewis believes in force, he believes in applied fear, he wants to rule.*

40 DISCOVERY

Gayle took a bus to the Playhouse Theater, where Ariel kept a tiny office. She was startled to see Ariel and Rikki sitting next to each other, watching the director instruct Richie in the role of Biff in *Death of a Salesman*. Gayle held back, but could hear the conversation. They were rehearsing a scene out of sequence, and satisfied with it, called it a day.

"Thanks for recommending Richie," Ariel said to Rikki. "I could cast him again. We're going to put on Ibsen's *Ghosts* next time."

"What's *Ghosts* about?" Rikki said.

"About errors and mistakes and regrets. Like all the plays I put on."

Richie came over, chatted a bit, and Rikki left with him. The other actors and the director left also. A stagehand shut off the lights. Ariel remained seated in the dark.

"Ms. Smith," Gayle whispered.

"You scared me!"

"I'm sorry. My fault."

"Not your fault. I'm jumpy." Ariel looked out at the darkened stage. The darkness felt darker. Then suddenly she said, "I feel sad every time I see you. You saw the whole thing. The secrecy, the sadness. Trinity's adoption."

"Trinity wasn't adopted."

"What are you saying?"

"Your daughter Trinity is actually Rikki Grover." Gayle said it in a hush, but it sounded like a thunderclap and Ariel recoiled. Gayle revealed Ann's lies, offered details. Her voice was barely audible, yet she felt as if she were screaming. Her hands were trembling. Her own troubles seemed minuscule by comparison. She described Rikki's foster homes in detail. Waves of guilt and horror were catalogued. Fear occupied her breathing.

"Did you tell Rikki any of this?" Ariel asked.

Gayle shook her head to say no.

"I can't forgive myself. I buried that child." Ariel drove Gayle to her trailer, and then drove to Ann's mansion. She pushed past a nurse to confront Ann in her wheelchair.

"Does Tom know how you destroyed our daughter?"

The silence seemed impenetrable. Ariel slammed her way out of the house, and went home to confront Tom. He listened to all of it. He shook his head. "If anyone knew what we did to Trinity—"

"Rikki, Rikki, Rikki! We did it to Rikki!"

"If this got out—"

"Tommy, I want to respect you—"

"Nobody would vote for me."

"This isn't about the election—"

"Not even—"

She stopped listening to him.

THERE WASN'T A NIGHT afterward in which Ariel didn't wake once or twice a night thinking about Rikki. She called up Rikki to discuss puppet staging and the scheduling of new shows for children. She asked Rikki if she had the time to work as a volunteer assistant to help manage the Playhouse Theater. Every time they met Ariel felt alive with a passion for truth, for revelation, for openness. She touched Rikki's arm when they talked, a fleeting butterfly touch. She winked if either one of them said anything remotely witty or humorous, trusting that humor connected them. Yet Ariel couldn't confess, couldn't admit, couldn't let go of the secrecy.

41 THE HOOKER

Rikki was driving Richie in the Audi Lewis had leased for her. She tried a soothing tone. "You'd like Lewis if you got to know him better."

"Our defender of public safety? He's a dick, a corrupt public official. He can afford to be so generous with you because he's betraying his public office."

"You're saying he's taking bribes?"

"Isn't it time for you to stop playing the innocent? The first thing an outsider moving to our town notices is the corruption. You've closed your eyes when it comes to Lewis."

"I want Lewis to love me."

"He's a killer. What's love have to do with it?"

"I sleep with him. He sleeps with me."

"Stop being so dainty. He fucks you."

"He fucks me."

"But not as frequently as before?"

"He's busy. He's the deputy mayor, he's the commander of—"

"The OP gang?"

"He watches out for me—"

"While killing others. He's the guy they would put in charge of the gulag, the concentration camp, the death march."

"Can we stop this? Can we please stop this?"

"All right, all right. I'll put on my happy face."

Richie segued into his latest gambit to win market share, hustling more carpet, more parquet, more oak, more tile, persuading customers to change their flooring right now, even this week, even if their existing flooring might last another generation. "I'm good at selling excess consumption."

"You like that work?"

Richie looked at the windshield. It was raining and the wipers swishing. "It sucks and it pays." He wanted to become the town's best known flooring vendor. That was the goal and yet it was empty of value. He wanted to have a friend forever like Rikki. That was true value. "Let me show you my store."

She went to see it, but the store wasn't what she'd expected. She saw a squat building, an ordinary-looking one-story building, and the paint on the façade was mottled from age and beginning to peel. The parking lot had been swept and several cars were parked in front. It didn't look like a rich place at all, and it disappointed her. Advertising had captured her. Bit by bit, by perfect staging, by Photoshop perfection. Everything ordinary and regular and human seemed somehow deficient. She had imagined a magic carpet palace, a place with bustling employees and well-dressed clients. She had imagined a steel-and-glass palace that Hayden owned on Black Mountain, a beautiful multilevel structure that had several cantilevered sections flying into space, and a stream captured in a culvert that rushed from under the house.

Richie wasn't troubled by her doubts, or the store, or anything else. He had an all-embracing willingness to give it a try, even if the chance for success was limited, even if globalization made him a retro local event. The magic had moved away from the middle classes. Hard work was a fool's errand. The magic resided in banking and Silicon Valley and the startups in Manhattan and Seattle and San Diego. It may be unfair, he thought, but history had passed him by. He was young but outdated already. Turn the clock back. Change the genes. He should have inherited his wealth. Most successful children fly toward successful careers on account of their parents and family, like Hayden had done, like Abbey was expected to do. Neither Richie nor Rikki had those fabulous parents to help them.

She had succeeded as far as she could on her own, and Richie had his optimism to fuel his dreams. She realized that he didn't want to remain in the carpet business. He didn't want to be the expert on the best way to power-stretch a carpet, how to kick in the corners on a staircase, how to keep carpet secure with tackless strip and how to clamp it down to a wooden or tile floor—nylon carpet, polyester and wool—he didn't want to be known for his flooring skills. She hoped his entrepreneurial energy would take him further.

Inside were rolls and rolls of carpet, the surfaces thick and plush, or knobby or shag-like, dyed many colors, or solid in silver or jewel tones or subtle earth tones. There were so many ways to make carpet that she wondered how people could choose what to buy. Consumerism reduced to the floor. It looked like hard work.

The carpet store itself was pleasing, with large carpet samples cascading over waist-high stands to give the effect of a colored waterfall, and wall racks were filled with smaller carpet samples with their color arranged as rainbows, but the work of fetching and throwing samples at customers' feet didn't look like fun.

Richie showed her the window banners shouting "THREE-DAY SALE!! THIS WEEKEND ONLY!!!" He recited, "Living room and dining room and hall. Wall-to-wall installation FREE with half-inch deluxe cushion." In an aside he whispered, "'Deluxe' is the cheapest stuff we can put down under the carpet." But an expansive gesture came next and he pivoted and danced across the showroom. He sashayed back and forth. She clapped. They couldn't ever have as much fun with anyone else.

"Hey," he whistled. "People get bored selling carpet. Minds go stale, mouths go dry, arms get sore, and knees hurt. So I dance to move the cobwebs."

"I've never seen you so happy."

"It's my own business! I won it! I own it. I earned it! I'm it! I've got to do somethin', brag a little."

"You change roles quickly."

"With every customer who walks in I get to play a new role. I'm a lady's man with a lady, a guy's guy with a guy. The show goes on. I think I'm better than most salesmen, and yet I'm insecure. I try harder. The days of small businesses are past, say the prosperous townies. They also praise shopkeepers like me, often working for mere wages. Minimum wages at that. We're in the age of metadata, mega-bosses, mega-policies, mega-laws, and mega-companies—large businesses dominate us—I feel like a thin vine holding on to a bare living. That's why I need you. We can make a go of it. We can go big."

"How big?"

"No, not just big, but huge! You'd be amazing."

"I'm afraid to be without money," she said.

"That's how we started, no money."

"I'd like to have money."

"I'll wave my magic wand. We'll have tons of money."

"You're a hooker," she said, "like I used to be."

"You're still a hooker if you stay with Lewis."

"What should I do?"

"Dump the guy. He's no good for you. You're too good for him. You're beautiful. You're fantastic. Our customers will love you."

"No one adopted me," Rikki said.

"Don't you remember? We talked about it. We adopted each other."

"You're a sweetheart."

"You're doing all right now?"

"Yes. But it's never the same when you grow up like I did. Everything is always conditional. I was born to be wary."

"That means we're meant to be partners. Do you think I belong? Deer Creek is organized by heterosexual twos: two to date, two to marry, two kids, two divorces minimum—"

She was swayed by his affection for her. "I love you too." He was her Knight of Malta who'd sworn a vow of chastity to be with the Lady Rikki. He wanted to see her more often; he wanted them to be together.

42 FIRE AND ASH

The fireplace poker was still hot after Hayden had used it. Ariel picked it up and poked the logs one more time. She scattered the hot cinders violently. "Our daughter could have been murdered."

Hayden startled.

Ariel swung the poker hard and hit the grate inside the fireplace. Sparks flew in every direction. She stomped on the ones that dropped to the floor. "I'm going to talk to her. This is homecoming. Our firstborn coming home."

"You're dreaming."

"Yes, I am."

"She's been in plain sight all these years, and now you show up to claim motherhood? She'll know something's up. I'm hearing that she's committed to Lewis and she knows that Lewis wants to destroy me. She'll know right away that what you're doing is trying to get back at Lewis, trying to use her to get him."

"You're so full of tactics, so big on strategy. What do you expect from me? Isn't love simple, undecorated, never so smart?"

"I love you," he said. "Aunt Carver isn't going to make it. She's drifting out. You slammed her hard. She's gonna be gone any day now."

"The damned bitch."

"Will you attend her funeral?"

Ariel placed the hot poker back onto its stand. "I'd rather go to hell."

43 GAYLE LOFTUS MUST PAY

Gayle Loftus couldn't pay Yoshiro, and wouldn't move out. The county sheriff still didn't have the proper authorization to evict her. Yoshiro hired additional security guards and stationed them next to the bulldozers and backhoes threatening her trailer home. She slipped past them, carrying the engraved silver box, and brought it to the BuyPawn store that Rikki helped to manage. They had talked about Gayle's financial troubles, and Rikki wanted to help.

At the store Rikki gave the heirloom a cursory inspection. It had a beautiful wrought edge, delicate and skilled craftsmanship, a velvet protective covering on the bottom. She saw the baby footprints but the store lights were at such an angle that they obscured scroll-like text and signature. She knew that it symbolized a secret stage in Ariel Smith's life, who'd recently taken a much closer and a more affectionate interest in Rikki's puppetry performances.

The store was crowded. Rikki made a point of not looking closely at every detail because she didn't want to make Gayle uneasy.

Gayle, for her part, was terrified even though Ann, buried in regal style, was dead. Gayle had already revealed the truth to Ariel, and had expected a blowup. Lightning, a hurricane blowing, emotions thundering, but nothing had happened so far, which was disappointing. She'd resisted telling Rikki partly because she believed that biology triumphed over nurture, and worried that once Rikki knew the identity of her true parents she would move closer to them, abandoning Gayle to old age.

Rikki was deep in thought too. The heirloom was a repository of one family's secrets that could hurt her best friend Abbey. It was impossible to imagine the box in a stranger's house, a catchall for keys or coins or whatnot. Rikki called Lewis and asked him to buy her the silver box. She quoted a much higher price than it was worth.

"Wow," he said. "That much?"

"For being such a shit to me."

"Babe."

"You can skip buying the ring and buy the box as an engagement gift."

"I leased you the Audi. I was going to buy you a ring?"

He hadn't gotten past desire, past intimacy, past the logic

of loins, and he wanted to keep it private. He gave her his credit-card number. She brought the deal to the store manager, who then okayed it on a straight ten-percent store commission, all the rest went to Gayle, and the box now belonged to Rikki.

She considered giving it back to Gayle. She considered returning it to Ariel. She considered what the box meant to Abbey. Her best friend didn't know that she had a sister shrouded in mystery, a sister who may be dead or missing, a sister her parents refused to identify or discuss.

The heirloom appeared to be a burden to everyone who had touched it, a container filled with secrets. Unable to give it away, Rikki stored it.

44 THE SPIRIT OF DEER CREEK I

That morning, Lewis stirred and stirred his oatmeal. The brown sugar swirls were beautiful, Rikki was beautiful—he couldn't leave the woman alone, which alarmed him. She rattled his self-control, preyed on his mind. He had gone into debt to lease her a car. He needed to find more money than his salary provided.

"What are you brewing?"

The voice was immediately recognizable—velvet and soft.

"Hi," Lewis said.

Yoshiro was with his chauffeur, Soto Cesar. Cesar went to the counter to order takeout.

"You remind me of a first sergeant I used to work for," Yoshiro said.

"You served?"

"Yes."

"Thank you for your service." Lewis nodded toward the empty chair, hoping that the Quiet Man would sit and grant him an audience. Yoshiro looked at his watch.

"You flying with the mayor?" Lewis asked.

"I gave up my seat. I'll drive out at my own pace. What's the Gayle Loftus holdup?"

"We're working on it."

"The Annex demolition permit?"

"A judge ruled we couldn't evict her yet."

"How much longer?"

Lewis noticed again that Yoshiro wasn't inclined to sit and break bread with him. Yoshiro tapped his wristwatch. "It's costing the city money not to have the Halcyon Annex up and running. It's costing me money."

Lewis hesitated. "Say, do you think I can tap the bank for a loan?" Yoshiro owned a majority stake in the Deer Creek Bank.

"How much do you need?"

"Sixty thousand to a hundred thousand?"

"Big spread."

"The high end is better."

"Can you speed up the Loftus thing and the demolition permit?"

Lewis said he'd check on it. Whatever unspoken agreement passed between him and Yoshiro didn't need to be put into a letter of intent. There was no wink, not even a nod.

"If all goes well," Yoshiro said, "we'll all make money."

"If it all goes well," Lewis said.

"Yes. We've presold eighty percent of the Annex condos."

"To Europeans?"

"Lambs."

Lewis smiled. "It's a loan. No funny business."

"No funny business." Yoshiro leaned forward. "You're next in line to become mayor."

"If something happens to the mayor."

"Not if but when. After you become mayor, you can then think of the loan as a campaign contribution."

"We're not doing anything illegal?"

"That's right. Nothing illegal. You need money to run for office. The Supremes say I can shout as loudly as my money allows me to shout. I can give you as much money as I want. Free speech. My money speaking for me."

Lewis stirred his coffee. He loathed the idea of running for office. He detested primaries, pandering politics, the rigmarole surrounding elections. He wanted to lead unimpeded by second guessers, the Monday night quarterbackers. In a perfect world he would have stormed city hall and occupied it. His troopers and the fanatic OPA operatives taking over. He altered his tone slightly—familiar, friendly, and encouraging. "Yoshi, I'm happy to have your support."

Yoshiro turned to leave and speaking over his shoulder, said, "See Stephanie. She's still at the bank. Sign the non-recourse paperwork and she'll have the amount deposited in your account overnight."

Non-recourse meant that if Lewis failed to repay the unsecured loan the bank wouldn't come after him. He would get the money free. Again, there was no wink. The deal was straightforward. Yoshiro was heading out, Soto Cesar a step ahead of him opening the doors.

Lewis phoned John Foster to ask if any seats had opened up on the mayor's helicopter. Foster told him that they were all taken, but if anything did change, he'd let Lewis know. In the meantime Lewis should plan on taking his own car or the chartered bus.

"Yoshiro gave up his seat," Lewis said.

There was a pause. "Let me talk to the mayor."

"Don't be a prick," Lewis said.

"Who's a prick?"

"I'm the *deputy* mayor."

"You left your civil-service protection when you took the executive promotion."

"What are you saying?"

"Hayden can fire you for mismanaging Halcyon planning."

Lewis leaned back in his chair. "You *are* a prick. I'm the best man the mayor ever had working for him."

"You're in Yoshiro's pocket. You should have blown the whistle to stop the Halcyon Annex, not pushed for it. We can't go on poisoning those Europeans. We need to fix the water contamination."

"Make it public? Reputations would be ruined."

"Deer Creek will recover, but your mentor, Yoshiro—he'll come out of it broke. I'll get back to you about the flight."

As the leader of the OPs and the head of the OPA Lewis effectively ran a rump political party as well as an unsupervised and unregulated secret-police agency. The analogy to Hitler's rise to power didn't escape Tag Orr. City council members had abandoned their constitutionally sworn duties to protect and preserve civil liberties. Lewis was more powerful than any Deer Creek executive, lawmaker or judge.

Lewis held his tongue. The wait was interminable, irritating, and disrespectful. Ever since Foster had come along Lewis had been losing influence with the mayor. The CEO of OmniMedia was only thirty years old, appointed as a dollar-a-year man on the city's payroll. The crown prince was treating Lewis like a second-rate underling. It chaffed and annoyed, an insult that burned. Lewis dreamed of the Century City he would found and lead. He would have the OP arrest John Foster, right along with Mayor Hayden.

45 GROWING UNCERTAINTY

Uncertainty was on the rise in and around Deer Creek. Abbey's father was more demonstrative and emphatic in his public speeches. She addressed him as "Mayor" in public just as others did. It was hard to say "Mayor" and "Dad" all in the same breath. John Foster kept pushing the idea that *Tom Hayden is married to Deer Creek.* Ariel explained it to Abbey: "When Dad is in on official business he's the mayor. When he's at home he's for me and for you." And that's the way it was at home, and at their Black Mountain compound.

Abbey was indifferent to political happenings and didn't understand the catastrophic events overtaking her hometown. She had a fifteen-year-old's excitable mind, blessedly and happily uninformed by current events. The audacity of ignorance marked her cheerful disposition. Only after she'd started collaborating with Rikki on *Sun and Shadows* did a broader awareness dawn.

"Where's the doll?" Abbey asked.

Rikki pulled it out of the puppet box. They were at the arboretum barn, beside the mottled mirror that kept their reflection antiqued in a golden frame, staging and photographing Rikki's escape from Stux.

"It's so small," Abbey said. It was eight inches tall and dressed in sequined jeans and a western shirt.

Rikki used a big voice to speak for the puppet—a garrulous whisky-edged pretend voice that made Abbey laugh.

They finished the shoot and lounged on the partially opened bales of hay.

"All those homes you lived in?" Abbey asked. "They're all so different. I was lucky to be an only child. Things never changed for me. I always got what I wanted. I learned to like things the way they were. I didn't want anything to change."

"I never stopped looking for something to change in my life," Rikki answered.

They locked their Janus coins. The mottled mirror caught their reflection. Abbey was a few inches shorter. They saw each other tenderly looking. Rikki brushed Abbey's cheek with her lips. "I'm not going to break your heart. Not ever."

46 THE SPIRIT OF DEER CREEK II

Memories are so goddamned short, the mayor was thinking. He had brought public amenities to Deer Creek, a golf course, a rec center sporting an Olympic-size swimming pool, a track, the Ice Palace. He had extended the free downtown shuttle service. He had pushed for bike paths and revitalized the industrial swamp.

What did he have to do with poisoned waters? Nothing.

It wasn't his fault the economy had fallen off the cliff. The council had requested a new budget projection and he had ordered a new budget projection, but he wasn't going to sit back and take abuse on account of the numbers going south on him. Lewis and Speaker Lott were gunning for him. He was almost sure of that.

Hayden had made a few mistakes. In his first term he had been against the red-light traffic cameras on principle. He loathed the feeling of being monitored, the feeling of being under surveillance as if in a police state. He believed in Milan Kundera's assertion that privacy was the indispensable condition for man to live free. He believed that human authenticity and autonomy is denied by government surveillance.

The cameras were sold to the city as traffic-safety devices that would save pedestrian lives, but that was untrue or at least unsubstantiated. The cameras produced revenue, as simple as that. Lots of revenue. Millions. In a region that prided itself for its "no new taxes" policies, records showed that most of the ticketed were out-of-town visitors. Typical first time offenders were older drivers who did not have the swift reflexes needed to stop in time for a short yellow light. Fuck the citizens who hated the cameras. They weren't getting hurt. It was outsiders shopping at the Deer Creek regional mall who footed the bills. Big money. But the frequency of accidents and traffic injuries remained the same.

Lewis loved the cameras. The OPs loved the cameras. The police establishment wanted total surveillance and control. Camera revenue funded the OP pension fund, and you couldn't win an election in town without help from city union members. The pious and the practical shook hands on the issue of surveillance, undermining George Washington, Thomas Jefferson, all those crazy guys. Hayden compromised his true beliefs. The digital world made all this easier, cheaper, more accurate—a world without shadows, everything was illuminated.

Citizens never stopped hating the traffic cameras. Never mind, Lewis was gung-ho for adding more cameras. His plan was to coordinate them with surveillance drones in a shift-overlay pattern that would provide 24/7 surveillance of the entire city. The pols claimed they were listening to the voters, but all they heard was their own heavy breathing.

The city had been incorporated sixty years prior as a developer's city, and developers came with backhoes and bulldozers and carpenters and electricians and myriad other tradespeople to chew up the five-acre lots. The local cows had to find pastures elsewhere. Then came a regional mall, big-box stores and the auto dealers. The nearby metro areas grew faster, fueled by high-tech jobs, and their real estate was expensive—but Deer Creek was cheap. The land was cheap. The homes were cheap. More builders came to build apartment buildings in the wake of subsidized public transportation. The die was cast—the look and feel of Deer Creek. It was an inexpensive place to live, and the local jobs, except for the wages paid to health service professionals, were mostly minimum wage.

Deer Creek became an amoeba-like commercial blot that had no central feature—the regional shopping center within its borders became the city's ideological center. But Hayden had changed the city by backing the Halcyon development. The health industry employed more doctors and nurses, physical therapists, sexual therapists, psychotherapists, counselors, and health-service workers than any other similar-size city.

The clash between old patterns and new had nearly vanquished the mayor. He had been an idealist, but then he needed to govern too. He wasn't the mayor of just one city; he was the mayor of many disparate fiefdoms collected under one roof. A bunch of subcultures, some underground, each with its own beef about losing out when revenue had to be cut.

Once again Hayden felt a palace coup brewing. Nothing specific—he saw it in the distance in people's eyes. Not since Hayden's first landslide election as mayor had he had a challenger. Hayden felt bilious, barely tethered at times. He saw John Foster outside the office trying to get his attention. Everyone wanted the mayor; everyone had a complaint. He felt his brow perspiring and it wasn't even warm in the building. He'd ordered that the thermostat settings be set for maximum economy.

What burned him more than the excessive city overtime pay wasted to animate the rolling eyes of young staffers Lewis had hired was the attitude of businesspeople who couldn't see past their money clips and palatial homes. Some of them were so set in their opposition to government that they claimed they'd never seen an official they couldn't learn to dislike. But nothing in his administration would function were it not for the dedicated civil servants coming to work each day. Absolutely nothing. This was no golden age for heroes. There was no James Bond to come down and save the day. The business guys would have to become warlords with private armies to protect their booty.

He tried to calm down. What the hell did Foster want now?

Foster entered and placed a cell phone in front of Hayden. It was on mute. "Lewis wants a ride out to the coast on *The Spirit of Deer Creek*. We have two free seats." At that moment Hayden could barely stand to be in the same room with any of his staff, let alone in a small helicopter, but he took the obligatory call and invited Lewis to come on the flight.

The mayor hiked his pants higher, tightened his belt, slipped on a cardigan, and was ready for his evening meal. Ariel was still at a commissioner's meeting. Abbey was staying overnight at a friend's. He was a tall man and carried himself gracefully as he entered the restaurant. He ordered oysters, a salad and a double scotch.

He saw Yoshiro approaching him. The man was smiling so broadly his teeth looked ready to fall out. His arm was extended in greeting, palm upturned to show he had no weapons. The guy would probably murder Hayden in a heartbeat.

"Yoshi, you like oysters too?" Hayden faced a man he did not trust. He was ready to get down to business with Yoshiro.

Part Five

THE FUTURE

47 HURRICANE RIDGE

The chartered bus, *Kalaloch Express*, left on schedule. Ariel was on board as were most of the city's officials. Hayden had asked her if she'd wanted to take the helicopter but she preferred to be with her commissioners. The itinerary had them touring Sequim, visiting Hurricane Ridge, and checking in at Kalaloch Lodge before doubling back to Port Angeles for a fishing charter.

Hayden delayed his helicopter flight to give him more time at work. At the last moment, he decided he couldn't bear being cooped up with Lewis in the helicopter. He called Chief Clapton and John Foster and said they were leaving right away. Foster told him he shouldn't alienate Lewis for no good reason. "Fuck Lewis," Hayden said. He didn't tell Foster that Lewis was dating the mayor's discarded child.

An hour later they were aloft in the *Spirit of Deer Creek*. "Call Lewis," Hayden ordered.

"What do you want me to tell him?" Foster asked.

"Tell him to go fuck a kite."

"Fly a kite?"

John Foster shrugged and called Yoshiro to confirm his departure by limo; he then called Lewis and explained that a pilot scheduling conflict forced the mayor's early departure and that he should hop a ride in Yoshiro's limo leaving later that day.

"You're a prick," Lewis said.

"What's new?"

The *Spirit of Deer Creek* caught up with the *Kalaloch Express* at Sequim. The pilot called the bus driver and asked him to meet the mayor's party at the helicopter's landing site. That accomplished, the mayor's party boarded the bus, and the driver took them on a tour of the lavender fields near Sequim, then on a side trip to Hurricane Ridge. Ariel's eardrums popped from the elevation as the bus climbed higher. The perilous drop-off on one side of the road was dizzying.

None of the select circle of top officials on the bus wanted to face their grim task at the seaside meeting. The agenda had not been published, and lower-level commissioners and volunteers like Richie hadn't been informed about the details. Ariel didn't want to leave Abbey behind, and Abbey had insisted on asking Rikki to come. Richie was a seat behind them. They didn't have the least idea that the other passengers were heading to the most secret meeting ever organized by Deer Creek officials.

Dr. Wilkin sat in the front of the bus behind the driver. The seat next to him was empty because no one wanted to sit next to him. He was nodding off to sleep.

Ariel and Hayden were at the rear of the *Kalaloch Express*. Hayden wanted to say something essential about his and Ariel's secret past, something special about having a secret daughter.

"You always knew what to do," he said.

She basked in his unalloyed positive view of her, but she saw herself in a different light. Her competitive nature got her into trouble. Fellow commissioners called her bossy. They said she was smart, tenacious, but those who opposed her said she was ideological and dismissive, even abrupt. Her inability to take advice sometimes cleared a straight path toward accomplishment, and other times it hobbled her. She was also loyal and attractive and used every shimmer of that attraction to help Hayden.

"What if it doesn't blow over?" she asked. "Our kids seeing each other and wondering why they look alike." The back of the bus was a sheltering cave, a protective asylum sheltered by the rows of supplies.

"Rikki is a lovely girl. She's intelligent—"

"We both want the best for the kids." Ariel's heart had nearly stopped at the sight of her two children together.

"Why can't we just admit the bad part from our past and get on with our lives and our kids out in the open?"

"Stop torturing yourself," he said.

They reached the Hurricane Ridge tourist area, the bus slowing and wheezing to a stop. The driver secured the brakes and opened the door to let everyone out. He said everyone needed to be back in forty minutes.

"I'm afraid to leave the bus," Ariel said. "I'm afraid to step out and be seen with the children."

Hayden looked at her. "The nose, the eyebrows?" He looked again. "Yes, the forehead too?"

"I'm frozen."

"They'll think something is fishy back here if we don't leave the bus."

"How can I face them together? What if—"

"They're not—"

"I can't—"

"As observant as you are," he said.

He stepped out into the aisle and motioned for her to follow. "Let's go."

"No. Please, give me a moment to breathe."

He kept holding his hand out. She took it and then gripped the backs of the high seats as she went forward. Stepping out on the pavement, she almost fell.

"Oh, hi, Mom," Abbey shouted. And more excited, "Meet my friend Rikki."

"We've met. The Sun and Shadow Puppets."

"Hi, Mayor Hayden; hello, Ms. Smith," Rikki said.

Ariel sent an air kiss. Hayden waved. Richie left for the men's room. Rikki adjusted the lens on her Nikon. "We're going to shoot an alpine glen," she said, and ran off with Abbey.

"That was easy," Hayden said.

Ariel took a deep breath. Her bright-eyed, beautiful, daughters charmed her. "What are we going to do about the children?"

ABBEY HAD WATCHED HER mother step off the *Kalaloch Express* and knew that something was wrong. It was so disappointing. Adults tended to ruin things. Her mother's eyes had turned blank. Shadowed, lined, almost night-like. She was usually encouraging, talkative and helpful, and now this troubled look. It wasn't like her. The distance in her eyes could have stretched several miles, and there was something in them close to fear. She wondered what it was about Rikki that had upset her mother.

She had hoped her mother would like her best friend, and now it looked as if it were otherwise. Maybe daughters and mothers weren't meant to share everything they feel and experience. Maybe Rikki would have to be on that list.

The bus driver blew his whistle, a ten-minute warning to board the bus. Ariel was one of the first to get back on, scampering, which was not like her, as if afraid to be seen.

Richie went back, too. But the alpine glen still beckoned Abbey and Rikki, a field with several kinds of flowers swaying in the light breeze and the color of the grass changing, shifting from light green to silvery. Rikki lay prone in the field, framing her shot. She could never leave an angle untried. She shot across the tops of the tall, fluttering grass and pulled the focus to fill the frame with the mountains in the distance.

Abbey felt wonderful. This feel-good feeling, a way of speaking without words, a way of intimacy without touching was not only perfect but unknowable, too. The bus driver blew his whistle again. The sisters ran to the bus.

48 OLYMPIC PENINSULA

The *Kalaloch Express* was cruising along, taking them through a photographer's paradise. The light of day was fading, but there was enough sun to silhouette the fir rising on a ridge to give the trees a golden edge, and just enough light on the surface of Crescent Lake to make it shimmer. The cedar trees and the fir were swishing by. Occasional boughs showed hanging moss and lichen streaking the north-facing tree bark.

Ariel rested her head on Hayden's shoulder. She had once thought that life was moving too slowly, and now it was running too fast. The wind grew louder, and the evening light seemed to fade faster.

The northern part of the Olympic Peninsula is a place of contrasting moods that change in the course of a year. When the sun shines on the summer lavender fields you can cut your own lavender, buy lavender ice cream and lavender soaps and lavender caramel candy. The fall brings clouds that gather around the straight and Salish Sea, and move inward to cover the fields turning to a silvery green and shades of gold. The winds usually pick up as you head toward the Pacific coast, and by the time you reach the ocean in the area of the Kalaloch Lodge, you've entered a season of storms and melancholy moods.

After the bus arrived at Kalaloch, some of the passengers were taken to a less expensive nearby motel. Richie and Rikki checked into their separate rooms and took a nap, showered, and, not especially hungry or eager to spend time with the secret contingent of Deer Creek officials, went for a walk on the beach.

"My carpet business is booming. I'd love to have you join me as my partner." He kicked a sand dollar and whistled. "Have you been hearing what I've been hearing?"

"Yeah, Dr. Wilkin's report." She'd continued her clandestine work with Dr. Wilkin, proud to help, becoming politicized, polarized, and eager to change Deer Creek.

"If the report gets out, we're all done for," Richie said. "That means you and me too, financially speaking." He accepted the inevitable, the forthcoming losses. What he couldn't accept was not having Rikki as his business partner.

They stopped near the water's lapping edge. It was past sunset now, the western haze still lingering on the horizon.

Both were caught up in their thoughts about the life they'd led and could have in the future.

ON ANOTHER PART OF the rocky beach Tom was walking hand in hand with Ariel. They enjoyed the beauty of the fading daylight and waited a while before turning back to the lodge. Most everyone had eaten and had checked into their rooms and cabins. A few were at the bar, and several others had pulled together a couple of tables near the windows and seemed deeply engaged in conversation. The place was lighted dimly. Tom and Ariel ordered a martini each, and then crab cakes they shared. There was something going on with the group sitting by the window.

Speaker Brian Lott had taken a commanding position among the participants. His back was turned toward Ariel and Tom. At the table to his right sat Councilman Ernst Riddle, a broad man with a crew cut, long sideburns and full lips. Across the way from him sat the new planning manager, Kirstin Powell, a slim, vivacious, dark haired woman in her mid-thirties. To Lott's left was an empty chair. Daniel Hix, a retired shoe salesman who had been a city councilmember for a dozen years, had just left it. Arriving to take Hix's seat was Mila Stone, recently appointed to serve the unexpired term of a departed councilmember.

Ariel watched the choreography of changing seats—as one councilmember left and another councilmember took the vacated seat. The musical chairs in government jobs had never interested her, except on hotly contested cultural issues. Deer Creek officials, the managers, and the regulators, legislators, executives, and government employees in general, no matter which party affiliation they declared, all seemed to join to the same union once they came to power. The public was not invited.

"What's going on?" Ariel asked.

He glanced toward the tables and smiled. The reason for changing seats was simple. A meeting of four councilmembers was a quorum that could pass laws. Thus the state required that any such meeting had to be announced and open to the public. In keeping with the letter of the law, four councilmembers didn't want to be caught sitting at the same table at the same time making laws in private. One left, another returned; there were never more than three.

Ariel asked, "Should you announce yourself?"

"To stop the plotting?"

"Yes."

"You can never stop the plotting."

Dustin Lewis and Yoshiro entered the lodge and took seats among the plotters.

49 TAG ORR

Unnoticed by the plotters, or Ariel and Hayden, Tag Orr had found a cozy two-top nearby. A planter with a fiddle-leaf fig secluded him from the plotters. He never spared his client's expense account when eating out of town. He wore a bib and was eating fresh, broiled lobster that came with a lemon wedge and a cup of clarified butter. Orr overheard the sniping at the political table.

He had enough information to make a solid report. Councilwoman Mila Stone had dropped out of law school and was beholden to Yoshiro for her employment. Councilman Daniel Hix was too old and too tired and too Lear-like to run for anything, but he had tried to do his best for the city. Councilman Ernst Riddle was a lout and had the support of the Norwegian and German communities who didn't know he was a lout. Speaker Lott was impossible to pin down. Among the four of them they could make any law and citizens be damned—that's how they'd passed the red-light traffic camera ordinance that the citizens hated.

Mayor Hayden got a mixed review, a chameleon. He had campaigned on a platform of open government and transparency and then changed his mind.

"We can do it," Riddle said. "We zone them out. We prohibit their kind of land uses."

Kirstin Powell was enthusiastic. Dustin Lewis nodded his approval. They were like two winking ducks approving each other's quacks. Yoshiro was the sphinx, silent. Hix was astonished. "We seize their buildings?"

"No, that's illegal," Riddle explained. "We simply prohibit them from doing the kind of business they'd been doing except by a conditional land-use permit. But we won't be granting those conditional permits. We give them a grace period to get out. We fix some legal triggers. We demand that they repurpose their buildings. But we know they can't get the bank financing to do it. Our goal is to get them out without having to pay them a dime, and then, if needed, when they can't pay their taxes, we'll deed the property to Halcyon Annex."

Orr made a note of it. City matters were simple and complex. Legal and illegal. Money dominated.

The Halcyon Annex project had sailed on like the doomed *Titanic* despite the city's mortal financial failings and poisoned spa waters. To help Yoshiro develop Halcyon

Annex Lewis had relabeled the city's land grab as a *revitalization* plan to give the impression that the city's rezoning effort was fair, a way to create jobs, improve property values, and build a future.

Orr wrote in his report that in practice this rezoning, for people like Gayle Loftus, was about as fair as being put in front of a firing squad. The rezoning made every non-spa use *nonconforming*, which meant that it was illegal at that location and needed special permission, a variance. But as Riddle had just explained, permission wouldn't be granted.

Without use permits the buildings were useless, tear-downs, because no tenants could use them. Yoshiro would swoop in to buy the devalued properties for pennies on the dollar. It was a grand plan, devious and intelligent—the city didn't have to spend a dime on eminent domain to condemn the properties before handing them over to Yoshiro. He rarely smiled but he was beaming now.

Lewis, too, was enjoying success. He had wanted to rule, he had wanted to lead, to seize the archangel's sword and chop off heads. To pay for his expanded police state he fought to keep the red-light traffic camera revenue, and fought for higher fees on permits and licenses, ordered OP run traffic traps—local bloggers said that if Dustin Lewis could, he would tax the sun for rising and traveling over Deer Creek, and each citizen would have to buy a digital punch card to pay for pissing in a Deer Creek toilet to fund the wastewater treatment plant.

"We can do that?" Stone asked. She'd been silent. "Aren't we breaking the rules?"

"We make the rules," Powell declared.

Riddle burst out laughing and Lott joined him. Lewis applauded. "If we can criminalize the height of grass in Deer Creek, we can do anything!" His face was alive with animosity.

Orr ate his lobster, enjoying the food more than the scheming. He believed in the rule of conscience and didn't think that laws were perfect. That was the reason he supported the people's constitutional power to nullify laws, a jury's absolute power to acquit a person on trial if the jurors think the legislators imposed a stupid law to deny freedom to its own people.

His grandparents were Auschwitz survivors. German law had made marriage between Jews and gentiles illegal and made murder legal. Laws in the South had made interracial marriages and homosexuality illegal, but the forced sterilization of blacks was legal. The law once made alcohol illegal. A law that financed the longest organized crime wave in American history started in 1970 as a "war on drugs" launched by President Nixon who famously declared, "I'm not a crook." Congress made marijuana illegal thus criminalizing a generation of youth. A war that continues today, still victimizing the poor, the young, the black, rewarding the criminal, and punishing good government.

The laws are so many today and the punishments are

so plentiful and so harsh that prosecutors can manipulate the charges leveled against a defended to such a degree that the odds against a defendant bucking a prosecutor to have his "day in court" are so absurdly low that no more than five percent of the accused, even if innocent, ask for a jury trial today. Prosecutors have assumed the role of judge and jury. The right to be tried by a jury of one's peers has been clobbered.

Laws. We have lots of laws, laws banning sex, laws banning marriage, laws banning a woman's "personhood" by making her a victim to a sperm deposited in her uterus—a modern version of male medieval seignory rules that allowed the master to have sex with his female servants before they marry.

There's nothing sacred about believing in the "rule of law" if legislators are wicked, greedy, corrupt, ill-informed, narrow-minded, stupid, or tyrannical. Conscience is still the best guide. Unfortunately, conscience too, though often useful, can be corrupt, ill-informed, narrow-minded, stupid and tyrannical. Edmund Burke once wrote, "The true lawgiver ought to have a heart full of sensibility. He ought to love and respect his kind, and fear himself."

50 RECOGNITION

Over the next two days everyone invited to Kalaloch assembled. None of the invited dared not come: the officials, the councilmembers and key staffers, even Dr. Wilkin, encouraged by Rikki set aside his doubts and came to confront his accusers with the truth. All told, about two dozen Deer Creek officials, lawmakers, and commissioners were expected to take the fishing cruise. On the free day before the cruise Rikki and Abbey and Richie set out in a borrowed car to scout the Olympic rain forest.

They'd heard that the *Twilight* trilogy had been filmed in Forks, but they later learned it was actually shot it in Oregon and Canada. This setback didn't trouble them but something else did.

"My concept could be all wrong," Rikki said. She hadn't

yet decided if her personal project was a straight up documentary, a comedy or a tragedy. In a comedy all should end happily in marriage; in a tragedy someone has to die at the end. Rikki scribbled more notes. She'd revised the photo narrative so many times that she could've had a dozen personal projects under construction.

"We're shooting out of sequence," Abbey said.

"Let's keep working on it," Rikki said.

Their affection for each other was everywhere and in everything, and had a half-life of forever. "Rikki an' me," Abbey kept saying. The two of them were like bookends—one without the other wasn't as useful.

Rikki's photographic series remained ambiguous, the stills and events dissociated from a central goal. She wanted her personal project to be lighter, airier. She wanted to rise above the dystopian clouds; she wanted to be Dorothy taking Toto out for a walk on the Yellow Brick Road. But the material kept demanding something else, darker.

Richie found a huge fallen cedar in the Olympic forest. The Spanish moss hung in sheets on the tall surrounding cedars. The bark seemed to be iron plated. Abbey changed into the white princess costume Rikki had made for the shoot. Richie helped her climb to the top of the fallen cedar. She moved gingerly to the middle of the uprooted log, her white costume swirling around her. "Don't slip on the moss," Rikki warned, clicking away with the camera. The Nikon could shoot eight-frame bursts in a second.

"Have you guys noticed how much you look alike?" Richie asked.

They looked at each other. One sister was still standing on the fallen log, the other sister below. It was unsettling and unexpected to see it. They'd ignored it.

"She's nothing like me. I was a hooker," Rikki said.

"You were a prostitute?" Abbey asked.

"A sex worker," Richie said.

"That's before I went legitimate as a surrogate teaching sex."

Abbey was silent.

"Well, but you guys *look* alike," Richie said.

They looked at each other again. Their eyebrows were beautifully pronounced, their eyes serene, their cheeks alive with days and summers into the future. They could stay in that mood of happiness undisturbed, seeing what seemed to be beyond vision, breathing slowly, never having to think or to worry, never alarmed, and together.

Their affection for each other was innocent, enduring and inviolate. They returned to Kalaloch and the next day the chartered bus took everyone to the ship.

51 SEABORNE

The pocket cruise ship had several decks and a huge pilothouse, a galley, food servers and hired cooks, and a bartender at an open bar. It was an expensive charter, the best available, and funded by taxpayers. Unknown to any of them, Tag Orr had booked a premium captain's cabin. He didn't want to be recognized and had boarded early and stayed out of sight.

Dr. Wilkin had a cabin nearby. He heard a knock on the door.

"It's me." It was Rikki. "I need to see you."

"Give me a minute," Dr. Wilkin said. "I'll meet you at the bar."

She went away. He pulled on a sweater. He was a man of science who worked on cause and effect, on continuity, bell curves, probability and statistics. Peer-reviewed medical journals had published several of his research papers. He had been a social man, and now he wanted to hide. The Deer Creek spa waters were tainted. Halcyon was a bad idea, and no one in town wanted to listen. He had become the enemy of the people in the city where he was born. They called him a traitor. He made his way to the lounge and sat next to Rikki. He patted her arm. She wore a diaphanous silk-sleeved blouse and had a cosmopolitan cocktail in front of her.

"Hi, daughter," he said.

"You always call me daughter. I'd be a hell of a daughter. I'm supposed to get you drunk."

"Right out of the Bible," he said.

"Did you hear what I said? I think you're in danger."

"I'll buy the drinks."

"You're not listening to me."

"Yes, I heard. You're supposed to defame me in some way to diminish my credibility."

"You need to watch out for yourself."

"I'll buy," he repeated.

"They say you're a traitor."

"It's true. I'm a traitor to profit. I've lived among my neighbors for forty years, and they're all saying that. Your boyfriend Lewis has his OPs hanging out near my home and office. There's a license-plate-scanning cop car outside. No one gets in or out of my place without the police knowing who they are and where they're going."

"Why are you doing it?"

"Whistleblowing?"

"They said you broke the law by threatening to release city secrets."

"They always say that. They always use the law to protect government misconduct."

"You're so calm."

"Thanks. I'll be okay."

He pulled a pamphlet from his hip pocket. It was a maroon-colored booklet. *The Constitution of the United States of America*. He skipped the "We the people" part, and read her the first and the fourth amendments.

"And you're not afraid?" she asked.

"Yes, I am."

His speech was slurred. He had been drinking in his cabin, but he ordered more. They chatted a while and when it became late he said he needed some shuteye. She didn't want to leave him alone. But he repeated that he'd be okay. He steadied himself as he pushed away, tottering, working to catch his balance as he left the lounge.

Rikki remained at the bar. She noticed Orr at a small table. He winked at her to indicate a wish to remain unrecognized, and she turned away. Lewis came up to her and took the seat Dr. Wilkin had vacated.

"You did your job. The guy looks stoned."

"He bought me a drink."

"How many drinks has he had already?"

"I don't know."

"I hope he's seeing double."

"I'm your honeypot plotter to get at Dr. Wilkin?"

He shot her a glance. "We can't help what might happen to a drunk."

"You said we're going to be a couple. You've turned against me, haven't you?"

He looked around the lounge to see if anyone was looking at them.

"You promised," Rikki said. He had said many things. He had said too many things. She fingered the glass in front of her.

"You're tops, babe."

"You would shoot me if you were a dictator. You would behead me if you were a king." She sipped her drink.

Lewis kept his ever-changing script secret. "I got Yoshiro to give you a raise."

"A raise for what?"

"Because you're the best." He wasn't looking at her.

"You're not drinking?"

"I've got to stay alert. The ship is taking swells from the Pacific."

"You know what Dr. Wilkin told me?" she asked.

"I haven't a clue."

"He said he would do it all over again."

"The fool."

Lewis excused himself and left her at the bar. "Don't

leave!" she shouted. He turned, looked embarrassed, and placed a finger to his lips to silence her.

Orr had observed it all and felt a disquieting anxiety. He got up and went looking for the purser. On the pretext that Orr was worried about his friend, they knocked on Dr. Wilkin's cabin door. No one answered. The purser unlocked the door and found the room empty.

52 LIGHTS OUT

Passengers were known to party most intensely on the first night out. The ship's captain was in the pilothouse at one a.m. when the first shout reached him. Later the captain wouldn't be able to recall who shouted, "Man overboard," a deckhand or a passenger. He believed there'd been a cry for help, but he wasn't sure. Even though he was cruising slowly there was no way to hear everything above the sound of the wind and the sea.

More shouts followed. He stepped outside the pilothouse, looking starboard. Four or five people were on the deck below, perhaps more. It was hard to tell since not all of the deck lights were working. Either they'd been unscrewed or burned out all at once.

He ordered a general alarm and the horns sounded from bow to stern. Several people were still fishing. No one could actually see into the black waters but they said they could feel the pull on the lines.

The missing lights—it turned out they'd been unscrewed—were a suspicious item in a follow-up admiralty investigation. Several people noted that the glare of the lights had bothered them when they were fishing and that they'd asked a deckhand to unscrew them, but they couldn't identify the deckhand from the pictures that were shown to them. In any case, the captain couldn't be sure who'd been on deck. He said several people appeared suddenly and then retreated.

His crew illuminated the sea with searchlights. The horns were still blaring. He stopped all engines. The searchlights scanned the empty sea, lighting the cresting waves. No one was in sight. There were no more shouts or cries for help. He swung full right rudder, brought the ship about and powered along the ship's own wake. It seemed like an eternity, those few minutes before the ship was doubled down on its wake. The searchlights were playing across the waters, port and starboard.

It may have been another five minutes before the crewmen spotted someone in the water. They lowered the lifeboat and sent it out to retrieve the passenger. The captain was lucky—often at night the person lost overboard couldn't be found, but they found Dr. Wilkin. It wasn't clear whether he'd hit the guardrail or the bulwark or flotsam in the water as he fell. A blunt force had marked his skull. No one came forward to say they had seen Dr. Wilkin fall overboard.

The captain called ashore before they returned to Port Angeles. The medics took Dr. Wilkin's body and the captain made a report. The *Kalaloch Express* was standing by, Yoshiro's limo, too, and the mayor's *Spirit of Deer Creek*. No one wanted to stay a minute longer. They didn't return to Kalaloch Lodge and the meeting was canceled.

53 DECLARING WAR

Tag Orr was methodical, but couldn't complete his report. Maritime law and death on the high seas are complicated legal and investigative matters that drag on and on.

Someone could have bludgeoned Dr. Wilkin, but that was only one scenario. Lab tests confirmed that Dr. Wilkin's blood-alcohol level had been high. It was likely that he fell overboard because he was drunk. It was also possible that the friendless man committed suicide.

A crewmember came forward to say that the first shout came from him, but there were passengers who must have seen Dr. Wilkin fall overboard before the crewman saw him in the water. Did the town's worthies hold their communal breath?

Every Deer Creek passenger who was questioned denied seeing anything. There was fog and there was booze, and even though the seas weren't rough, ocean swells rocked the boat. Passengers' memories remained cloudy; the seas they remembered were rougher. The captain, his memory freshened by the mate's log, reported occasional gusts but otherwise nearly normal conditions. The reports contradicted each other: one said fog, the other said gusts.

A crewman said that he might have heard at least two or three voices speaking immediately after Dr. Wilkin fell. He wasn't sure. But the crew had checked all the cabins for safety reasons and found that most of the passengers weren't in their cabins. No conclusions could be drawn from that. The lounge had still been open and a solo guitarist, Soto Cesar, was playing. Why was the man performing during a general alarm?

Something startling happened soon after Dr. Wilkin's death. He had no close relatives and had appointed his bank as the executor of his estate. The bank official in charge of the estate released Dr. Wilkin's statement, which expressed a fear for his life. Dr. Wilkin asked that in the case of his death, his report, *Poisoned Halcyon Waters*, should be released to the public. The executor notified the deputy mayor and asked where it should be published.

The city of Deer Creek went into high gear to suppress the report, claiming that Dr. Wilkin had stolen privileged city information that he wasn't authorized to share. The claim was outrageous, but the court put a gag rule on the report until legal arguments could be heard.

A month went by without incident. The Ice Palace opened. An unexpected front came in from Canada and froze the smaller lakes, earlier than anyone could remember. Abbey persuaded Rikki to go ice-skating on the lake in order to drag her away from the morose mood she'd been in ever since Dr. Wilkin's death.

"Don't go out on the deep," Rikki pleaded as Abbey headed out, gliding across a patch where the white, scaly ice surface changed to a translucent green-blue color. The ice whispered tiny crinkling sounds as she skated farther and farther, and then the ice began making ominous cracking sounds. Rikki swooped in just in time to grab her and skate them back to safety as a huge crack behind them filled with water.

"You can't go getting killed on me," Rikki said.

She was distraught over Dr. Wilkin's death, but Lewis, rising in his powerful role, wouldn't talk to her. He froze her out, not responding to her texts or voice messages, not answering her calls.

She dropped Abbey off at the mayor's house and went home. She inspected the silver commemorative box with Ariel's engraved thank-you note to Gayle Loftus. She felt honor-bound to return the expensive item to Lewis. She went to his office, startling him, and placed the commemorative box on his desk.

"Our engagement is broken," she said.

He stared at her blankly. "Engagement?"

She felt trapped, rejected, fooled, and despondent. The box sat on the desk along with an OP manual, two empty glasses, and a carafe of water. He inspected the heirloom she'd just handed him.

"What's the matter, Dustin? What?"

He held the lid opened. His fingers shook a little as he tapped the silver box. "I needed proof, and now I have it." He stroked the heirloom as if it were a kitten. "All the political troubles Hayden will face will fly out of this box."

"What are you talking about?"

"I'm going to be mayor."

"But you have to run for office."

"Not me. I'm never going to run because I couldn't get elected. I'm going to get the job when Hayden resigns." He dug into a file he kept in his desk and showed her a document. His brow was flushed and sweat ran down his sideburns. Precious minutes were ticking. He pointed to the name-change document. "Stamped by Superior Court." He was triumphant. "You didn't know this, did you? Rikki Grover is Trinity Smith. These are *your baby footprints*."

"You're insane," she said, unwilling to take it in. "Abbey is my sister?"

"Once this gets out—"

The room was spinning. Rikki's heart was pumping. The impossible came hurtling down. The similar features they shared, the speech and gestures too. The silver box seemed to levitate, sparkling unevenly in the office. A shallow and uneasy feeling crept closer to them. Rikki seized the box. He grabbed the box back. He was going to be mayor. He didn't have time to waste. Perfectly done, he told himself. Perfectly done.

54 SISTERS

The thrill of discovery was quickly submerged in a feeling of doom and rejection. Rikki avoided Abbey and Abbey couldn't tell what had gone wrong. Rikki stopped putting on her puppet shows and hung up when Ariel called for an explanation. Abbey begged her to go ice-skating, and finally she'd accepted.

A rink bully, the tubby Benson boy Abbey had dated and then stopped seeing, spun in front of them, throwing ice crystals across their path and into their faces.

"Don't fight him," Abbey said.

The Benson boy spun around and shaved more surface ice into their faces, and Rikki and the bully were into it at once. She landed a right hook. He threw himself forward to seize her in a bear hug. Skaters scattered every which way to avoid them. Rikki felt blood streaking along her forehead and into her eyes. She got a leg free and kneed the bully, collapsing him onto the ice.

The encounter ended as quickly as it had begun.

Abbey and Rikki started skating again, encouraging each other to be confident. They skated large half-moons, gliding from left to right and back again. They circled and circled the rink. Rikki's hand was at the small of Abbey's back and it felt as if they'd always been together conversing with silent words, silent moods. But their roles were suddenly reversed. Abbey felt she had to protect Rikki, who seemed suddenly frail, almost broken.

There was a gated bar where adults bought beer and bullyboy from Benson was drinking out of a paper bag. The music stopped and the flat-screen TVs in the concession area went blank. "Breaking news," lighted the TV screens a moment later and an announcer exclaimed, "This just in! Mayor Tom Hayden has resigned! The mayor says he will not allow the most important people in his life to be dragged through the mud just so he can stay in office."

Rikki felt a sharp pain in her side. The pictures of her father, the mayor, left her cold.

More headlines blasted onto the rink's TV screens. The announcer offered the latest: "A scandal in the mayor's office! The mayor's illegitimate daughter surfaces as a prostitute. His long-term girlfriend admits that Hayden fathered their secret daughter. Our reporters are looking to interview the woman."

A TV van had pulled up to the Ice Palace, and a camera crew and a reporter entered. The reporter held a picture of Rikki.

Rikki saw her picture. There was nothing to say, nothing to do—she wanted to escape the attention, get away from the camera lights, the questions, and the startled faces. She wanted privacy; she wanted to be left alone. She hid her face and ran, tripping over Abbey. The cameraman got a long shot of them struggling to stand. At the same time John Foster and Chief Clapton arrived and grabbed Abbey, taking her with them. Rikki was left behind in the churning media attention.

Pictures of Ariel flashed on the TV screen showing her at ribbon cuttings and at the Ice Palace gala, and more pictures of the mayor and Abbey. There was so much noise, so many questions. A reporter kept poking his mic into Rikki's face. She was afraid of all the attention, afraid that her life was all gone, smashed to bits. She ran from the reporters, first to the ladies' room and then out the window. She drove away, escaping the glare of attention. She stopped to text Abbey: "I love you. I miss you. I'm holding my half of the Janus coin to be complete with you." She didn't return to her house and crashed at Gayle's place.

55 CHAOS

John Foster delivered Abbey to the mayor's house. Her father was seated in a chair by the fireplace. "I'm glad they've found you." He'd been looking out the window, waiting for her to come home.

"Where's Mom?" Abbey asked.

"We're sending you to Seattle until this blows over."

"Where's Mom?"

Hayden gave his daughter a closer look. He could be rough and smooth in the space of several minutes, but he was always energetic, optimistic, smiling, ushering, cajoling, and in motion. Now, though, he wasn't any of those dynamo things. He was gentle. "Well," he said after a moment. "It's all coming out."

"How come you threw away my sister?"

"It's a long story," Hayden said.

"You let those people trample her."

Hayden motioned for John Foster to come closer. The headmaster in Seattle was the mayor's old friend. Foster had made all the arrangements, smoothing the way with a large building-fund donation. "You'll be staying with a fine family. The mother plays violin for the Seattle Symphony. The father does research at the Battelle Institute."

"I need to talk with Mom. When is she coming home? I need to talk to her."

"Your mom and I discussed it. We've decided what's best for you."

"I want to talk to her."

"She's not coming home."

"You're breaking up?"

"We're not going to live together any longer."

"You're separating?"

"We decided it's best for you."

The fact was as explosive as learning that Rikki was her sister. Abbey's life was in disarray, shattered. A patchwork of strange emotions and unexpected painful jabs stabbed at her heart. It was like dying, she thought. Nothing was worthwhile, nothing solid, nothing to live for. "I'm not going to leave without Rikki. I'm not going to *leave*."

"Young lady, you've got a long trip ahead of you. We've hired a tutor to make sure you're up to speed once you start school." He paused. "I need your cell phone."

Abbey read Rikki's message: *I love you. I miss you. I'm holding my half of the Janus coin to be complete with you.*

"I'm not leaving without my sister."

Hayden took Abbey's phone. "You're going into seclusion. We don't want anyone to know where you are." He looked out the window and saw a TV truck arriving. Foster pulled the shades closed. "John is going to take you out the back way."

It was the end of everything.

Two waves went through Abbey, one paralyzing her, one enraging her. How could they do such a thing, dump Rikki? It was the end of innocence, and it fueled a self-destructive urge, a sudden wish to hit back by hurting herself.

That night in the safe house across town, where Foster also took a room, Abbey feigned calm, but the moment Foster stepped out to the 7-Eleven for a newspaper, she innocently asked her hostess if she could use the computer to check her Facebook page.

"Oh, I suppose," the woman said.

Abbey logged into her page and posted a suicide note. She signed off, "Rikki, I love you. I'll love you forever."

The message went viral but in the morning she was in no mood to kill herself.

Foster drove her to Seattle."I got hell from your father over that suicide note. They've got an army of reporters looking for you."

The couple housing Abbey kept the phone and computer

away from her. She saw only bits of TV. Foster became Abbey's watchdog, working as driver and bodyguard, escorting her to and from school, keeping her sheltered from the media that had descended on Deer Creek. She'd never been this isolated before. She didn't know that Rikki had taken her suicide note as genuine. She didn't know that Rikki was texting her, text after text after text.

RIKKI READ AND REREAD Abbey's suicide note. The absence, the silence . . .

MailOnline, the British scandal paper that features American crimes, posted Abbey's Deer Creek Prep photo with the headline "Missing girl feared dead after father is disgraced." The New York *Daily News* online, and also *Huffington Post* picked this up.

Gayle Loftus released a statement that she hadn't meant to be the cause of any trouble. The Seattle paper published a picture of the ex-mayor dodging reporters. A sidebar explained that "the mayor's disgraced girlfriend" had resigned as the chair of the arts and parks and recreation commission. Reporters had ferreted out hospital records identifying Ariel as Rikki's biological mother.

The revelations paralyzed Rikki. She couldn't talk to her mother, or her father. She couldn't talk to Abbey. Her therapist was off on a month-long tour. Lewis refused to take her calls. Gayle was endlessly apologetic and on the point of emotional collapse. Rikki blamed herself; she should have been wiser, smarter. Her fixation on Lewis had been disastrous. What did she expect to get by returning the box to him? Had she subconsciously expected him to change his mind about their relationship? Her emotions had been all confused. She should have given the box to Ariel or Gayle. Her confidence lay shattered. She was once again unlovable, a discarded child, the unwanted woman, a pariah. She was angry too, betrayed.

56 ADVICE AND CONSENT

The city council moved into high gear and passed a resolution demanding a full investigation. Interim Mayor Lewis announced that the Order Police security forces were working to expose the ex-mayor's alleged wrongdoing. Rikki felt responsible for all the bad news. She contacted Chief Clapton, who by all accounts still felt badly that a policeman, even if not under his direct command, had fired the lethal shot that killed Mr. Clark.

"What can I do for you?" Chief Clapton asked.

"You know me?" Her voice faltered.

"Yes, ma'am."

"If a former client attacks me and forces me to have sex with him, is that rape?"

"Yes, ma'am."

"What do you need to arrest someone?"

"A complaint. Evidence."

"What evidence?"

He explained the evidence collected in a rape kit. "Do you have a complaint to make?"

"No," she said. "Not yet."

"Everyone is equal under the law. I want you to come to my office and make a complaint. I can help you."

Rikki thanked him, ended the call and used her smartphone to get on the Internet. She Googled "rape kit" and found several companies selling them. She ordered one from Minnesota and paid for next-day delivery.

The following day she was out the front door as soon as she saw the FedEx delivery van. She took the package from the driver and went inside to study the instructions and count the items delivered. Then she went to see Richie at the carpet store.

57 SUN AND SHADOWS

"I've been calling you, and calling you," Richie said. He hugged Rikki for a long time. "You're going to come out of this okay. You're going to be my general manager."

"You're a sweetheart," she said.

"Let's just do it."

"Yes."

"Yes? You mean it?"

"Maybe."

"You were never a 'maybe' person. You were either all in or all out."

"Yes," she said.

"Come on! Let's get some life into you. Who the hell cares about your parents? We've got our own lives. We have a business. I'm all here for you!"

"I've always loved your enthusiasm."

"Well cheer up, then."

"Cheers," she said, swallowing the word. "I brought you my personal project series." She had a large, heavy portfolio. "Abbey is dead."

"That's not at all clear," Richie said. "Hayden is telling reporters that she's in seclusion."

"She's dead," Rikki insisted, tightening the ribbons that tied her portfolio. "My ex-boyfriend is responsible."

"He's a dick. He always was a dick."

She handed him the bulky portfolio.

"Where are you going?" Richie asked.

"Oh, here and there."

"You're my partner. You can't go far. Let's stay in touch."

She took her cell phone out and looked at it. She switched it on.

He came closer. "The battery is almost dead."

"Yes," she said.

"Charge it so I can call you."

"Maybe."

"Come on, I need to hear that Rikki spirit!"

She smiled wanly.

"Where are you going?"

"I have a date."

"How about after your date?"

"Maybe the arboretum."

"The arboretum?"

"Yes."

He knew she liked working late. "I'm going to call you. If you don't answer me I'm going to start looking for you."

"I'm okay. It's okay. Everything is okay."

"I'm worried. I'm going to keep calling you. If you don't answer me after your date is gone, I'm coming after you."

She kissed him goodbye.

58 SEDUCTION

My dearest Dustin,

It was so beautiful between us before all this happened—

will you see me again the way we were?

Love, Rikki

Lewis was now the most powerful man in the city. He came over and Rikki set a plate with baguette slices and several kinds of cheese in front of him. He wolfed the bread and cheese as she prepared the main course. Her voice was low-pitched yet giddy.

She smiled and smiled to encourage him. A sudden fear came over her: what if anger or alcohol killed his desire? What if her weight loss had made her too gaunt to be sexually appealing to him? She wore silk, and her scent was delicate. She called him her sweetheart, her lover.

Her false testimony drove a spike into her heart. The man in front of her was responsible for Dr. Wilkin's death, and Abbey's suicide. The emptiness was all. Stricken with grief, she'd nearly stopped eating. Overcoming her queasiness, she'd prepared grilled salmon over sautéed spinach with a side of mashed potatoes. She assembled the food on the dinner plates as he ranted about Chief Clapton.

The beeswax candles were lightly scented with a honey. She set the dinner plates on each side of the lighted candles. She watched him eat. She had a fire going in the fireplace, and several pine logs were crackling.

He was blowing off steam about the police chief, who had declined to arrest a councilmember, and he was railing against the district attorney for refusing to seek a grand-jury indictment against Yoshiro's competitor.

"I'd fire Clapton," Lewis said, "but it wouldn't smell right with him being so close to retirement."

Rikki wore layered white lace that rose above her knees. Her makeup was barely noticeable. The lightly blue eye shadow made her eyes glow in the candlelight, and she had positioned fifteen candles around the room to honor Abbey.

Lewis spoke with his mouth half-full; he was so excited to be mayor. "We need an iron hand at the helm."

"That's you—you're strong."

"That's right."

She barely touched her plate, but after he'd eaten, she led him to the bedroom. She ran a hand along the coverlet to smooth the surface. He got undressed; she did, too. He started making the moves. His passion was quick, leaving the evidence.

She paused a moment, thinking, calm, and prepared herself. She imagined her childhood nightmares of killers lurking, werewolves attacking. The vision was intense. Fear of The Killer consumed her and her breathing quickened. She screamed, striking Lewis, gouging his face, ripping her fingernails along his back. He jumped out of bed, his cheeks bloodied, raked by her fingernails.

He was half-crazed and in pain. "You're an insane mess!" He wiped his face on her bedsheets, staining patches scarlet. He called her several names as he pulled up his slacks. "Look what you've done, look what you've done!"

He slammed the door on his way out.

The werewolves were gone, the fierceness tamed, the childhood Killer vanquished. She remained in bed, exhausted, afraid that Lewis might return with the OPs, arrest her and beat her. She clicked the bedside table lamp to a brighter setting. She reached under the bed and retrieved the rape kit and spread the swabs and the collecting envelopes and the disposable gloves flat on the sheet. She took the first swab from her vagina. She was disappointed that it didn't show much color. She touched the bloodied bedsheet to make the second vaginal swab pink. She was pleased with the result and marked it separately.

The evidence under her fingernails was easier to collect.

She removed the skin she'd gouged. She found what might be his pubic hair, and saved that, too. Her panties were next to the bed. She picked them up and tore them and wiped them against the bloodied sheet. She placed them in a sample bag. She spotted Lewis's handkerchief. That went into another sample bag.

Then she dressed in a long skirt and a checkered work shirt. She read the note she'd written earlier. It explained how Lewis had refused to return the key to her house. She'd addressed the note "To whom it might concern." She crossed that out and substituted "Dear Chief Clapton." She asked the police chief to seek justice for her.

Surveying the rooms, she realized that the cheese plate and all the candles and the dinner plates were a problem, suggesting a welcoming evening, a passionate half-hidden affair. She churned the food in the garbage disposal, snuffed out the candles, and collected the remains of dinner and put them in a shopping bag. She studied the kitchen and the tiny dining area carefully. She racked the dishes and the glasses in the dishwasher and started a cycle.

Her cell phone rang and she saw that it was Richie. She didn't pick it up. She felt no guilt and had no qualms. She was avenging the deaths of Dr. Wilkin and Abbey. She gathered the DNA evidence and reread her note accusing Lewis of raping her. The snuffed candles and the empty bottle of wine went into a neighbor's recyclables. She packed the rape-kit samples in a shopping bag and left for the arboretum. She purposefully left her cell phone at home and drove to the arboretum, attentive to traffic to make sure that she wouldn't be pulled over. That aside, her mind drifted into a pleasant state of emptiness.

She used her staff key to unlock the gate, parked inside and locked the gate. She walked through the humid section of the greenhouse, enjoying the passionate flowers blooming and the moss-covered rocks and tropical plants that looked like torn drapery. The hydrangeas that were planted outside the greenhouse—so many varieties, so many shapes to the leaves. In the summer some of the blooms were wafer thin and floaty, floral solar systems, while others were large and round or triangular and pendulous.

She left the greenhouse and went to the barn, where much of the transplanting was handled—the seeds and sprouts. The smell of hay was appealing. She noticed several varieties of Mondo grasses that had been brought in for a membership fundraiser.

There were plenty of materials to work with. The sisal rope was thick, but some of it was mildewed and perhaps weak from the mold and rot. No matter—it should hold. She cut a length and fashioned a noose.

59 THE ARBORETUM

The barn held several antique wagons that were restored and saved for display at public events. One was a buggy made of leather and polished woods, and it had a whip stand on the driver's side. The barn had an electric hoist used to move bales of hay and pallets loaded with potting soil. The hoist's master control had an up-and-down button. She stood in the front seat of the buggy and checked the distance she had to fall. She lowered the hoist's hook and tied the noose to the hook. Then she stood on the seat of the buggy and placed the noose over her head.

The moon was out and a dull light created a luminous atmosphere. She removed the noose. She took a finishing nail from the workbench and used a garden trowel to spike the letter addressed to the police chief to the buggy seat. She set the rape-kit samples on the seat.

She wanted to spend more time with Abbey. She climbed down from the buggy and made a bed for herself among the bales of hay. The barn odors were ripe with life. The sadness she felt lifted slowly. The sadness was only the fog of living on earth. The hay prickled against her skin. An owl in the barn hooted. That made her laugh. Mice were making a home in the barn too, and that didn't bother her either. Everyone and everything had a right to live, and a right to die. She dozed and dozed and woke and lay awake.

The dawn light brightened slowly, creeping higher. She was rested, and ready. She climbed onto the buggy and once again eyed the distance she had to fall before her neck would snap.

She was so thin that she feared she didn't have enough weigh to end her life quickly. She saw a basket of stones that had been painted with funny faces to entertain and attract children at the next fundraiser. She climbed off the buggy seat, found a gardening tool belt and filled it with smiling stones. She strapped the belt around her narrow waist and climbed back up.

Alert to the unknown hope of eternal existence, she rubbed her half of the Janus coin until her thumb and forefinger were so warm that she felt the fusion of souls, uniting her with Abbey. She prayed for her sister's help in getting to the other side painlessly.

There was no place on earth she'd rather be that

moment than there, forever thinking about Abbey, being with Abbey, hiding from the world of whispers whispering sin and censure and shouting hate. She unfolded a copy of Psalm 23 that had been her keepsake, her decisive security, and read it aloud:

The Lord is my shepherd; I shall not want.
He maketh me to lie down in green pastures: he leadeth me beside the still waters.
He restoreth my soul: he leadeth me in the paths of righteousness for his name's sake.
Yea, though I walk through the valley of the shadow of death, I will fear no evil: for thou art with me; thy rod and thy staff they comfort me.
Thou preparest a table before me in the presence of mine enemies: thou anointest my head with oil; my cup runneth over.
Surely goodness and mercy shall follow me all the days of my life: and I will dwell in the house of the Lord forever.

"What's going on?" Richie asked. He'd seen her parked car and climbed the locked gate of the arboretum to look for her. "You didn't answer my calls." He froze. "What are you doing?"

"Richie?" A peaceful aura surrounded her.

"You told me, you told me you're going to call me, that you're going to keep your cell phone on."

She took a step toward the edge of the seat and bent her knees to spring forward with force.

"No, no, no!" he shouted. "You're my best friend."

She jumped, tucking her knees close to her body.

He grabbed her and pushed her onto the buggy's footrest. They clung together like two reeds tangled by the wind.

60 JANUS, GOD OF BEGINNINGS AND ENDS

At the hospital trauma center where Richie brought Rikki that morning, doctors sedated her and a nurse used a rape kit supplied by Dr. Wilkin's clinic to collect additional samples.

A few hours later Chief Clapton showed up at the mayor's office with two officers. Mayor Lewis gestured for them to stay out. "I don't have any time for you, Chief. After all the effort we did to suppress Dr. Wilkin's report, another whistleblower has gone against the court's gag order and released a copy to the press."

"Sir, you're under arrest," Clapton said.

"What?"

"You're under arrest."

Lewis raised his hand to stop the chief from entering.

The two officers seized his hand and whipped him around to handcuff him. The judge declined to release Lewis on his personal recognizance, scheduling a bail hearing for the following week.

A YEAR AFTER LEWIS'S arrest and trial, several unanswered questions nagged Tag Orr. The final anonymous payment had compensated him for a follow-up report, and he'd delayed it too long. He made one more visit to Deer Creek. His wife said that he didn't know his client, and he had already done more than anyone could have expected. "When are you coming home?" she asked. The unspoken answer hung between them. He was several pieces short of completing the puzzle. He couldn't let go. He realized that if this had been a mystery film, viewers would be unsatisfied. He still didn't know who'd hired him, and wouldn't find out until Tag Orr had completed his interviews. He didn't know if Dr. Wilkin had been bludgeoned to death, jumped overboard or fell because he was drunk. Orr underlined the last point he'd made in his report to his anonymous client: the lineup of people who wanted Dr. Wilkin dead could fill a scroll.

The man reading the report, Tom Hayden, was now the president of a nonprofit organization. He hadn't been thinking about obstructing justice or betraying a lawful investigation when he'd hired Tag Orr. It was a preemptive election-year move. Hayden wanted to know what dirt others could fling at him. He wanted to know what fellow politicians could discover about his personal life and twist into a toxic sound bite to undermine him. He could then defend himself—explain the circumstances, change the details, suggest alternatives to give the story a favorable arc.

It took months to uncover all that had happened. Many facts had been scattered around for the public to nibble on, but the essential truth had remained hidden under several layers of doubt and official denial until Dr. Wilkin stepped in as a whistleblower. The city's health tourism had been built on a lie—the spa waters were unhealthy. Deer Creek Democrats and Republicans and Independents alike had conspired to hide government misconduct in order to keep the town prosperous.

The U.S. Army Corps of Engineers was called to fix the sewage plant that caused *E. coli* to bloom. But the harmful chemicals in the soil—it turned out that the abandoned battery-manufacturing facility and the ancient chrome-plating operation had been leaking chemicals into the soil for years—couldn't be easily cleaned up. There wasn't a tourist in sight, and none were expected. The shine was gone. The spas closed and the professional health providers left for jobs elsewhere.

The blazing historical moment in Deer Creek's Halcyon glory had corroded and the city collapsed. It couldn't cover its civil servants' underfunded retirement plan. Yoshiro was in bankruptcy court. His fabulous wealth-producing loan-shark business wasn't sharking fast enough to offset the mega-millions he'd lost on Halcyon. Gayle Loftus remained in her trailer park home. There were so many vacancies in town that the new owners reduced her rent. Brian Lott was now the Deer Creek mayor, and Dustin Lewis was in prison serving ten to fifteen years.

Rikki wasn't cross-examined at his trial. Lewis's lawyers had gambled that they had a better chance at acquittal by not questioning her. The jury had taken only forty minutes to come back with a guilty verdict. The defense team is appealing the verdict by claiming that the prosecution hadn't turned over exculpatory evidence.

Ariel had moved to San Francisco to take a job with the San Francisco Museum of Modern Art. Richie and Rikki moved also, and now own several carpet stores in Seattle. Abbey went to college. She and Rikki talk with each other every day.

There is something both satisfying and incomplete in all this. Public accounts are often incomplete. Officials redact all they can from the records. You don't know enough. Witnesses commit perjury. Cops lie on the stand. Officials mislead. Authorities get it wrong. People keep changing their minds. You have to guess. You have to do your best.

The takeaway from these events offers no golden standard of wisdom or justice. If vengeance is sweet then life is uncertain and justice a frail creature easily frightened out of existence.

After Tag Orr's final visit to Deer Creek, Gayle Loftus drove him to the airport. She told him that Rikki had sold her pictures at a gallery show in Seattle. He was happy to hear it. Tranquility in human affairs is often hard to locate.

Gayle stopped at the departure curb lane, unrolled a letter-sized parchment from a slender tube she'd been carrying, and handed it to him. "It's a copy of Rikki's artist statement. She wanted you to have it."

> *The* Sun and Shadows *series is based on real life, the artist's life, a real city, and if you like hyperbole, "true facts." The family and city exposures employed in my photography reveal and question what's often accepted as true. I hope that the truths that settle your life will have greater clarity than the truths that had settled mine.*

He read the statement, and unsure what to say, he said, "Thank you." He got out of the car and took his backpack from the rear seat. He waved goodbye, picked up his boarding pass from the airline agent and boarded the plane to fly home to hug his wife and children.

Acknowledgements

I'VE HAD THE GOOD fortune of a childhood spent in Europe, teenage years lived in Brooklyn, New York, military service in Anchorage, Alaska, and family life thereafter in small American cities. I owe a debt of gratitude to the citizens, civil servants and community leaders in these small American cities, who provide the soil and the seed for much that's so striking about our nation's energy and vitality.

The emotional content of any story is always hard to pin down accurately. But had it not been for my daughter, Lisa, adopted at the age of thirteen days, who is now the devoted mother of two children, and my biological son, Andrew, a paramedic and firefighter serving a small city, and had my wife and I not experienced their lives in our life—the themes in this novel might never have occurred to me. In addition, the chances are fair that none of my books would have surfaced from the vast ocean of the unknowable without the steadfast support of my wife, Donna.

I'm grateful, too, to have had the help of publishing professionals associated with The Editorial Department, among them Doug Wagner, Amanda Bauch, Beth Jusino, and the ever-masterful Morgana Gallaway. I wish to thank my friend Kelly Leslie for designing a series of visually striking book covers, and Rachel Anderson for RMA publicity. I especially wish to thank Emily Cooke for her compelling insights that doubled my work, but served readers better. Any deficit in the work remains mine. To everyone and for everything, I give thanks.

A NOTE ABOUT THE AUTHOR

Photo by Gediminas

The Lithuanian-born American writer HOLLAND KANE is the author of the novels *Deer Creek*, *Winter Reeds*, *Morning Light*, and the forthcoming memoir *Car Palace*. He spent his childhood in Europe and his teenage years in New York City. He served with distinction in the U.S. Army Signal Corps. Since leaving the service he has fled the sins and pleasures of corporate life, jousted with journalism, edited a literary magazine, flirted with bankruptcy, and prospered as an entrepreneur. He holds a Master of Business Administration in finance, and a Master of Fine Arts in fiction, and lives with his wife in the Pacific Northwest.

Visit him online at **WWW.HOLLANDKANE.COM**.

Winter Reeds
by Holland Kane

"Kane spins a fascinating web of discoveries and intrigue, and the surprises don't stop until the very end."
— *Kirkus Reviews*

Documentary filmmaker Mike Harrison moves from New York City to a remote Northwest town to research an infamous car dealership fire. The generation-old, unsolved arson left two people dead, and if Mike can solve the mystery, he'll have a career-making movie. He's distracted though, by beautiful Katie Ames, a fellow New Yorker who's come to Hallmark County with her mentally handicapped brother, to piece together their own complicated past.

Katie's dating an architect who was tangled up in the dealership arson. The man is obsessed with Katie, and threatens her when she tries to break up with him. The next morning, the police find his dead body.

Mike and Katie are outsiders in a town where the popular Sheriff Trout is a law unto himself, and citizens live under constant surveillance ... But there's a story to be told: one that ties the arson, the dead architect, the sheriff, and Katie's missing family together into a devastating small-town scandal.

Winter Reeds Print ISBN 978-0-9858293-0-8
Winter Reeds Digital ISBN 978-0-9858293-1-5

Morning Light
by Holland Kane

"A story of loss, ethics, and forbidden love."
— Kirkus Reviews

Seventeen-year-old David's mother is dying from cancer when he turns to her best friend—the beautiful, emotional dancer Emily—for comfort, which one afternoon turns into passion. Their affair is brief, but it comes with a consequence: she becomes pregnant.

Emily's devout Catholic husband has stopped sleeping with her in a dispute about birth control, so there's nowhere for the lovers to hide. Results crash around like lightning strikes as David tries to woo Emily, and Emily tries to hang on to it all: her imperiled marriage, her breakout career as a choreographer, her unborn child, and David.

As the award-winning novelist Carol Orlock observes: "In this exploration of a modern woman's search for love and fulfillment, Holland Kane sheds light on the dark places our dreams can carry us, places we never meant to go."

Morning Light Print ISBN 978-0-9858293-3-9
Morning Light Digital ISBN 978-0-9858293-4-6

CPSIA information can be obtained
at www.ICGtesting.com
Printed in the USA
FSOW01n0254040315
5459FS